Uncharted Horizons

Emily Harper

Contents

Prologue

"Don't you think it's a little strange of you to keep staring? I mean I get it, I'm hot but learn how to control yourself hun. Wouldn't want your eyes getting stuck now would you?" Iris sassed.

"You know being from El Salvador and all staring could get you killed" she continued on with a smirk.

"Oh please, humble yourself, I was just admiring the beautiful young lady across from us while our door is still open" Harley muttered.

"Whatever. First you budge your way into my section when I specifically told them I wanted this class all to myself then you torment me, now I have to spend this whole flight with you. Fucking wonderful" Iris huffed looking away from the girl trying to occupy herself with her phone until the plane attendants came with her meal.

"Damn right and I'm going to fuck with you the whole time until you show a little respect, how's that sound?" Harley rhetorically asked as if she was giving Iris an option anyways.

"It sounds horrible, how about you be a little useful and give me a tour of France through out my whole stay. You're obviously from here and every tourist needs their own little personal tour guide. How's that sound? Your accent gave it away if you didn't know already." The feisty girl teasingly whispered in Harley's ear.

"Oh yeah and what's in it for me?" Harley suspiciously questioned.

"You get to be around me my whole stay, duh!"

It wasn't like Harley was gonna reject anyways.

Showing a hot, feisty and classy girl the in's and outs of France doesn't seem so bad. What could could possibly go wrong?

Love. Thats what could go wrong.

Chapter 1

5 hours before flight.

Iris POV

"Seriously your daughter could walk in at any moment" I whimpered as she made her way down my neck.

"It's fine it's not like she could hate me any less. She should be on her way back home soon" the woman reassured as she pulled my shirt over my head.

"Okay but hurry, I can't miss my flight" I told her as she kneeled down to tug off my underwear.

She fucked me everywhere from the floor to the bed even in front of the window because apparently wanted everyone to see how good I was getting fucked.

To her knowledge I would never come across whoever witnessed our quickie.

2 hour later

I finally made my way to the airport after my little visit with Sylvia.

To say I was worn out was an understatement.

I'm taking this trip to France as a vacation from work since I tend to overwork myself.

I'd rather occupy my time working and making money than being at home doing nothing.

I booked first class which should guarantee no one sitting by me.

Apparently France is one of those countries you go to to spend it with your significant other or to find love.

Love is least of my concern, I love being single and being able to do whatever and whoever I want without having to worry about how it would make someone else feel.

The woman from this morning was just someone I'd met a random day at a store.

She was mediocre.

Her accent intrigued me plus she's older and I love older women.

Who knows maybe by some miracle i'll be interested enough in someone to peruse them. Though I doubt it, people disappoint me.

I finally checked my bags and made my way through security with only 30 minutes left to board the flight.

I swear security lines are unreasonably long.

It's either someone taking up the space of the belt and holding up the line or it's just a ridiculous amount of people trying to fly at once.

Last minutely I decided to grab a few snacks before I boarded and when I arrived at the gate people were beginning to board.

When I finally made it to my section I buckled my seatbelt getting ready to relax and close my eyes when suddenly a flight attendant came up to me.

"I'm sorry ma'am but this is a full flight and the only other available seat is next to you" the middle age women informed me causing my brow to raise in confusion.

"Okay? I booked and bought this section and it's classified as private so why would you book her on this flight knowing there would be no space for her?" I rhetorically asked the woman knowing she wasn't responsible for who did and did not get placed on this flight but the moral of the story is that she could've gotten on the flight after this one.

"Ma'am I apologize but there is nothing we can do about this unless you would like to rebook your flight for a later time or date you're going to have to be seated with this young woman for the entire flight. Please make your decision quickly we need to get going if we're going to be on time." The flight attendants monotone voice was singly coated with annoyance.

"Fine." I agreed as she went back to get the girl.

A few minutes later a tall curly haired woman took a seat next to me after throwing her carry on into the overhead bin. She didn't say a word to me after she buckled her seatbelt looking up at the flight attendant improving the safety procedures.

Not that I'm complaining.

I'm pretty sure she felt my eyes roaming her since she turned towards me making eye contact.

She's nice looking I guess.

I adverted my gaze—scrolling through my playlist and closing my eyes as the song West Coast by Lana Del Rey played.

Her songs never fail to make me feel better.

Iris Rosales, 24 an interior designer who lives by the power of manifestation.

A girl from El Salvador who migrated to Texas to make a better living for her family.

A girl who saved her first 6 paychecks to buy her parents, abuela and abuelo who all lived under the same roof a bigger and better house in one the nicest neighborhood in Salvador.

Her family were her number one supporters when it came to everything.

From liking women to wanting to move to the United States to have a better life.

Iris was a very respectable, humble and genuine woman.

Anyone would be lucky to have her.

Chapter 2

Iris POV

It's been about an hour into the flight and our first meals were being served.

The woman next to me made me want to strangle her.

I swear she was purposely sighing and moving around every 2 minutes in attempt to annoy me because she would look at me right before she'd do it or she'd shift towards me.

"Sigh in my ear again I swear I'll open the emergency exit door and throw your ass out without a second thought" I gritted through my teeth all while keeping my gaze ahead.

"Go ahead, the air pressure would just suck you right out with me. Then you'd really be stuck with me" The annoying thing jokingly retorted.

I wasn't fucking joking.

I rolled my eyes;ignoring her as i pulled my tray down. I was growing impatient and grumpy from hunger.

The flight attendant finally placed our meals down which consisted of mashed potatoes, a little ass steak and asparagus.

I placed a napkin on my lap and tucked another into the collar of my shirt, I began cutting my steak praying it was the slightest bit seasoned.

Finally bringing the steak up to my mouth chewing I hummed pleasingly enjoying the taste of the lightly seasoned steak.

Within 10 minutes I devoured my meal feeling sane and full and obliviously not wanting to be bothered.

But did I get that wish?

No, no I did not.

"So, what's your name?" The annoying creature asked me.

I ignored her, pulling my laptop out of its sleeve getting ready to go over the blueprint designs for this company who hired me to design their lobby after my trip.

Before I could even edit any of my work my laptop was being shut closed causing me to slowly turn my head towards the annoying piece of space.

"What. The fuck. Do. You. Want." I quietly hissed at her—trying to not disturb the other passengers.

"So feisty, what's the problem? Who broke your little heart?" She fake pouted while pointing at my heart.

I immediately swatted her hand away.

"Touch me again and I'll kick your ass."

"Awe the little accent. How cute" she teased shifting comfortably back into her seat staring out of the window.

I don't how I'll last another 7 hours with her.

Within a few minutes I unfortunately felt bad.

Maybe I should try to be nice to her, it's not her fault she exist.

"I didn't mean to be so rude." I mumbled.

"It's cool, atleast you're self aware you can't resist me" she answered in her seductive french accent.

Wait no, not seductive.

Not seductive at all.

"Your cockiness is making me nauseous" I scoffed rolling my eyes.

She didn't reply but was making faces at the girl across from us.

She eventually got up—following the girl across from us who's been blushing and looking her way for awhile now.

At least someone's getting some type of love and affection around here.

But, that's my fault for acting like a bitch most of the time.

No one wants to put up with my emotionally unavailable ass.

Not even myself.

Chapter 3

Iris POV

I was halfway asleep by time the French girl came back with a halfway unbuttoned blouse with her lips between her teeth.

The random girl she obviously fucked followed behind her minutes later with a flushed—beat red face and fucked up hair.

More fucked up than how it was when she stepped onto the plane but that isn't my business.

Her actions caused me to roll my eyes.

She made it just before small snacks were being passed around.

Her annoying ass doesn't deserve to eat.

"You shouldn't be hungry now should you?" I asked her.

"You reek of pussy by the way" I covered my nose in fake disgust.

"As if, you're just bitter it wasn't you" she shrugged to herself and even then her annoying smirk stayed on her face.

"Not that it's any of your business but you aren't the only one who got some" I smirked right back feeling amused by her shocked expression she managed to mask within seconds.

"Wow you actually said something interesting" she answered.

"Whatever go ahead and occupy yourself as you were doing before and leave me alone" I dismissed her as I zoned out.

I swear I felt her hard ass stare burning through my skull.

Deciding to catch her off guard I pretended I didn't notice.

Then I finally said something "Don't you think it's a little strange of you to keep staring? I mean I get it, I'm hot but learn how to control yourself. We wouldn't want your eyes getting stuck now would we?" I perked my brow up in amusement though she only continued to stare.

"You know being from El Salvador and all staring could get you killed" I continued emphasizing the word 'killed'.

"Oh please humble yourself, I was just admiring the beautiful girl across from us" The dark haired girl chuckled.

"Another one? Someone's on a roll" I mumbled to myself though she definitely heard me "The least you could do is shut up for the next 6 hours. You'd been pushing my buttons since i even heard of you and i could only assume this is going to go in one ear and out the other."

"Damn right and I'm going to fuck with you the whole time until you cave in and admit enjoy my presence" She only continued to look at me with her annoying smile.

That was up until a very useful idea to pop up inside my head.

"Or maybe, You be a little more useful and give me a tour of France through out my whole stay. You're obviously from there and every tourist needs their own little personal tour guide. Your accent gave it away if you didn't know already." I told her giving the best convincing smile i could muster up hoping she'd agree.

"Oh yeah? What's in it for me?" The French girl questioned.

"You get to be with me throughout my whole stay, duh." I enthusiastically said.

"What makes you think I'd take some random girl I met on a plane who i by the way, don't even know the name of to some of my favorite spots?" She rhetorically asked in a more serious tone causing me to sigh.

"If you can fuck a random girl you just met on a plane you can show me around but fine—Iris, It's Iris. Iris Rosado" I told her hoping she'd just say yes regardless of how we interacted with one another hours earlier.

Silence filled the air as she carefully looked me over in thought.

The flight attendant came around then came around to collect the trash and even then the woman next to me hadn't gave me an answer.

Her silence gave me time to think of what i really wanted to gain from this trip.

To have fun and enjoy myself or mope around about a life I long for but don't have.

Chapter 4

Iris POV

"Now that that's out of the way, what's your name?" I asked raising a brow.

"I don't think you're ready. My name's too sexy for you" Her cocky ass smirk made another usual appearance but I knew she was joking which in the end made me scoff.

"You're so dull, we'll have to fix that chérie" When I tell you i have no idea what that meant but it almost made me swoon, I meant literally.

"Just fucking tell me already pendeja" I puffed my cheeks out in frustration.

"Okay, okay. So bossy" She raised her hands in defense.

"Harley Monet."

"See, told you it's sexy. You're drooling sweetheart" she winked.

"Cocky asshole" I whispered but loud enough she could hear.

"You know I was kidding right? I don't mind touring you even if you are a stranger" The women who's name I now know as Harley stated.

"No, you're right. There's no telling what you might do to me.. you might try to kidnap me or something. Even worse kill me" I dramatically pondered gasping into my palm.

"You best believe if I really wanted to I'd be trying harder to lure you into my nonexistent trap but go on, tell me about yourself sweetheart" Harley's annoying but luring accent spoke.

"Nope, I told you my name first so you tell me about yourself" I initiated.

Harley just softly smiled and nodded placing her finger under her chin as if she was deciding what details about her life she would like to inform me about.

"Well for starters, I'm from Marseille, France but live in Paris for work" Harley told me while I sat and listened without interrupting her.

"I'm an only child."

Now is that really surprising?

"I'm a real estate agent and I so far have sold 14 properties recently and I was in Texas looking to buy more property to renovate and put for up for sale" She continued.

"Back at home I have a cat who I'm sure would love to meet you" Harley directed a gentle smile at me.

I never took her as a animal person.

"Your turn chérie" The French woman insisted.

What can I say? I don't want to let her on about my life at home but I want to be fair. Maybe I could just tone it down so I don't let her in on too much.

"As you know, I'm from El Salvador and I'm also an only child, I send my family checks every so often to help out and bought them a nicer home on the safer side of the country. When I moved from there to Texas it was really hard for me. I mean I'm used to violence and shitty places but seeing other cultures and different people of ethnicities made me grateful to be able to experience life outside of Salvador" I shrugged my shoulders.

"And what about your love life?" Harley curiously asked.

"Let's not get into that" I scoffed mentally gagging.

"Fine then, do you like women?" The curly haired girl questioned.

"Oh sweetheart."

I love women.

Chapter 5

Iris POV

"I love women" I told the French woman who appeared to be curious about my sexuality.

"But don't think I just go around labeling myself, I'm too young for that, I like who I like" I added.

I always had this idea in my mind about what gender I liked and finally deciding to come to terms with one sexuality and stand by it, but I stood by the fear of feeling attracted to someone who didn't follow under that spectrum. I didn't want anyone thinking I was confused or experimenting, I don't want to have to keep coming out as bisexual if i end up following in love with a boy or pansexual if I fall Inlove with someone who doesn't label themselves as either I rather just live my life label free.

"I would ask the same but I'm pretty sure we both know the answer to that considering you did whatever you did with that gringa" I rolled my eyes.

"You're such an ass but of course I love women, I wouldn't be talking to you if I didn't nor would I have joined the mile high club" She shrugged.

"Humble yourself before I do señorita."

"What could a pretty face like yours possibly do poupée?" The French woman teased knowing I understood nothing.

I playfully rolled my eyes at the woman.

She's actually not as bad as she seemed to be.

"What's the plan for when we land? We have about an hour and a half left" I asked curious about where she would be taking me.

"For starters I'm sure you need to convert to some euros so we'll get that handled then I'd take you to your hotel or wherever you're staying and make sure you arrive safely. After that we could maybe meet up the next morning for breakfast and begin our little tour, you okay with that?" Harley listed.

I still couldn't believe she agreed to this.

"That's sounds amazing, Harley."

"How long do you plan on staying chérie?" She asked.

To be honest I haven't booked my flight back home yet, I'd be leaving when I decide I'd had enough of Paris.

"Haven't decided yet, whenever my body has had enough of the atmosphere I guess" I shrugged.

She hummed in response.

"Why Texas? Out of all the other cities you could've moved to."

"I don't really have a good reason, I mean it's plenty of opportunities and people I guess. I love the weather and diversity and all the new things I get to try and do. And why haven't you moved out of France yet?" I questioned the dark haired girl who started running her finger through her curls.

"Just as you said, I don't have a good reason either. France is my home and I'm used to it but I wouldn't mind moving away for a change. I rather not move alone though."

Harley continued "I always wanted to move to move somewhere tropical or full of nature like Hawaii or Washington only con about Washington is the weather."

"You?"

"I never really thought of moving again after Texas but I love nature and seeing greenery such as trees and flowers, Hawaii seems nice though but expensive as shit" I responded answering her question.

"Definitely opposite of what i thought you'd say but don't think about the cost think about the experiences."

"You should know better than to judge by first impressions. I'm pretty unpredictable" I joked.

"Oh I know, you're just an exception."

I rolled my eyes listening to the pilots inform us we'd be landing soon and to buckle our seatbelts.

And my vacation starts now.

Chapter 6

Iris POV

After finally landing that 10 hour flight my ass was so sore and felt flat.

I waited for my luggage and as I was scanning the room I saw Harley talking to the girl she did god knows what to but Harleys eyes were on me.

I rolled my eyes and looked away shaking my head.

I'm not waiting on her to finish talking to that gringa.

Perhaps I'll go out tonight and explore the city.

I finally spotted my luggage and began reaching for it but a tan slender hand beat me to it.

And that same hand belonged to no other than Harley.

"I didn't know you were done talking to your girlfriend, but thanks anyway" I retorted reaching for the handle that got shoved away from me as soon as I reached for it.

"I'll carry it, let's go" The French woman told me brushing off my remark as she began walking away with both our bags.

Any other time I wouldn't let anyone tell me what to do but she has my belongings so I'm obviously going to listen.

I followed her into a taxi hurrying inside as it started to lightly rain.

It took about 30 minutes to get to my hotel.

Paris has no lanes and people just drive everywhere and around each other without a single honk and Harley seemed to think it was funny when I'd think we'd hit someone's car or get into a accident.

When we finally arrived Harley got out first and walked around the car to open my door for me with an umbrella in hand as the driver grabbed my bag out of the back.

I carefully exited the car as she closed the door behind me.

I leaned against the car looking up at her lingering gray eyes which made me feel nervous, she just stared at me her eyebrow lifting occasionally.

"I guess I should get going before the rain gets worse, thank you, for all of this" I motioned towards the taxi.

"Trust me, It's nothing."

"But i am relying on you to meet me at the Les Deux Magots cafe at 9am" She was practically telling me to be there.

"I'll be there Harley" I lifted myself off the car.

"You should go before the rain gets worse and you get soaked" Harley moved from in front of me.

I nodded mumbling a thanks and grabbed my luggage walking towards the hotel's lobby door.

I looked back seeing her staring at me, I shook my head and entered the building receiving my room key.

I checked the time seeing it was only 7pm so I would nap for awhile then go out.

After my nap I showered and dressed in a very fitted white dress with heels.

I did my makeup and clipped half my hair neatly in the back.

I decided against a sweater since it'd ruin my outfit.

I'd rather freeze.

After finalizing my look I left my hotel room walking down the streets of Paris looking for any place with a sign of a party.

A few minutes later I came across this night club that was packed with people in line.

While I was checking my surroundings taking note of where I was a girl called out to me.

"Qu'est-ce qu'une si jolie fille comme toi fait toute seule ?" A woman in the front of the line with her other two friends called out to me.

"I'm sorry I don't understand" I felt embarrassed coming to another country and not knowing the language.

"I figured, why don't you stand in line with us. I don't want your feet hurting standing in this line all night by yourself" The taller women said to me.

"I'm Andi or you could just call me whatever you'd like" The stranger added in her guttural accent.

It's reminds me of Harley's except Andi's isn't as alluring as hers.

"Iris. I'm Iris." I told her as she lifted the rope for me letting me in front her.

"Thank you— you didn't have to" I smiled at the girl.

"No worries jolie, let's go" Andi guided me into the club with her hand on my bare lower back.

We spent hours drinking dancing and grinding against each other.

She even started kissing my neck and eventually started making out with me.

After saying goodbye to her friends after partying for a few hours she insisted on taking me home with her but I altered the plan and made her come to my hotel.

Women can be serial killers too.

In the elevator she couldn't keep her hands off me so when we got inside the hotel room she guided me to the bed gently pushing me against it while still attacking my neck with kisses that would definitely become hickeys.

Andi pushed herself between my thighs grabbing onto my boobs but she suddenly stopped.

"I'm sorry I should've asked before— is this okay with you?" She asked concerned.

"Andi it's fine keep going" I begged her before I lost all sorts of sudden horniness.

She immediately continued pulling my dress off which left me basically completely naked besides my underwear.

She kissed down my neck and down to my collar bone latching onto my nipple causing me to capture my lips between my teeth suppressing a moan.

After giving the other nipple the same attention she lowered herself between my legs placing my legs onto her shoulders.

Andi lowered her head running her tongue inside and over my slit slowly, causing me to arch my back off the bed with my head thrown back.

She toyed with my clit for awhile then replaced her tongue with her thumb and came back up hovering over me capturing my lips as she rubbed my clit in slow circles.

While toying with my clit two fingers were inserted inside me causing my legs to widen and mouth to gape while staggered moans came and pushed through my lips.

Her pace fastened and she lowered her head back down latching onto my clit while I tangled my hands in her hair pushing her face closer to me as I moaned her name.

Her strokes became harder and quicker consequently I gripped the sheets closing my thighs around her head grinding myself against her tongue feeling my release heighten.

"Jouis pour moi, jolie fille" Andi commanded in hoarsely in her accent.

Within a few seconds I was cumming on her fingers and came multiple times in her mouth.

Round after round we were each other out and didn't sleep till' the morning.

I really hope tonights actions don't take a toll on me tomorrow.

Chapter 7

Harley POV

I've been waiting on this damn girl for about 20 minutes now.

I should've asked for her number, for communication reasons only.

I haven't ordered yet not wanting to be rude but I'm getting sick of waiting. I'm fucking hungry.

Just before I was about to get up and leave the café bell rung signaling someone entered the business.

Not even bothering to look that way I continued to annoyingly fidget with my fingers.

"Sorry I'm late, I come across some things last night" Iris exclaimed.

"From the looks of your neck I'm sure you had and wonderful and eventful night" I dryly responded.

"Shut up."

"Why haven't you ordered already? You didn't have to wait on me" The girl asked.

"I have manners but trust if you weren't here by now I would've left" Iris bit her lip nodding and picked up the menu looking confused immediately after.

"Sorry, this cafe doesn't believe in translated menus for foreigners. What would you like?"

"A cappuccino and toast is fine" She started doing the random lip bitting and eye contact again.

The server came up and asked for our orders.

"Bonjour, elle prendra un cappuccino et des toasts et pour moi je prendrai un jus de pomme et des toasts français. Merci" The server nodded and collected our menus before walking away.

Iris thought I was oblivious to her staring while I ordered.

"Enlighten me on your night since getting fucked is far more important than our plans today. I hate tardiness" I playfully glared at her.

Iris rolled her eyes "Well after you dropped me off I took a nap then walked to the nearest night club, that's about all" She shrugged her shoulders brushing me off about what i was really asking about.

I guess we'll pretend the hickeys aren't there.

"Anything specific you'd like to do today?" I began slouching in my seat.

"I was planning on seeing the Mona Lisa" Iris made slight eye contact with me.

"At the Louvre Museum. Fine with me aslong as you didn't say shopping."

"Oh we're doing that too. One of these days atleast" The girl exclaimed grabbing her utensils as the waiter approached us with our food.

We ate our light breakfast and had a slight disagreement on who should pay in which I won in the end.

I took her to the get her money converted to euros.

An hour later we were in the museum walking around as I told her all the history I knew of the architectures and paintings.

And finally we walked up to the Mona Lisa oil painting.

In person it's small as shit.

After senseless rambling about the things I learned in school about her I turned towards Iris.

"Life back then seems so interesting and nostalgic but very strict" Iris's silvery voice replied still taking in the information.

"So about meeting this cat of yours?" She grinned dragging me out of the museum.

We drove to my apartment and as soon as I unlocked the door I heard running paws against the floor.

Esme began getting the zoomies and running all over the place trying to play with Iris after she smelt her.

Iris bent down to scoop up the cat as I closed and locked the door slightly grinning at them getting along.

"She's so fucking adorable, makes me wonder why I never adopted a pet" she geeked baby talking Esme and giving her belly rubs.

I walked into my bathroom inside my room and began washing my hands and changing.

I walked around my island pulling out pots and pans and ingredients to make French onion soup.

"If this is your way of letting me into your bed it's not working" she moved all her hair on one side before sitting on my couch playing with Esme.

I shook my head smiling to myself and began cutting up the chives and onions.

Within 30 minutes I was finished and made a quite fancy presentation for me and Iris.

I called her over.

As she approached and sat down at my island stools she seemed speechless.

"No one besides my family has ever cooked for me" she was practically drooling.

"Oh just wait till' you try it chérie" I checked Esme's bowl making sure she had her dinner.

"Okay maybe I lied, this is definitely luring me into your bed" she moaned as the spoon entered her mouth.

I playfully rolled my eyes sitting down.

This girl is something else.

Chapter 8

Iris POV

I woke up the next morning in a fairly above average sized room in a comfortable queen sized bed with dark green accents.

It took a minute to realize where I was because I knew damn well it wasn't my home or hotel.

I checked under the covers to see if I was still dressed in my clothes from the night before but I had on a shirt that went mid thigh.

I huffed and threw myself back into the bed grabbing my phone seeing a text from the woman I seen before the trip.

Sylvia M. - How's France treating you? I miss you.

- It's been great so far. I'm sure we'll see each other when I come back.

Sylvia M. - Definitely. I want to see you, call me later?

- Sure.

I threw my phone down curling up in the covers.

I really don't want to get up right now and I hope Harley isn't a morning person.

As soon as I dozed off the covers were being yanked off of me.

And I sadly had to open my eyes to Harleys face.

"Wake up I have to go to a meeting and you need to get new clothes, so wake your ass up" The French woman blabbered.

"Fucking fine, atleast I'll get uninterrupted sleep there" I huffed noticing Harleys eyes lowering every so often.

She bit her lip and turned away walking to out the door.

"Come get me when you're ready" she walked out.

"Fucking perv" I mumbled.

I got dressed in slightly loose joggers that were neatly folded on the night stand.

After we walked to her car we made small conversation.

"How do you feel about meeting me at a club tonight after work? Unless you have pla-

"No I'd love to go" I cut her off putting my seatbelt on as she drove off.

"Don't you think life would be a little easier if we could communicate in other ways?" she gripped the steering wheel tighter.

"If you wanted my number you could've just asked" I dramatically batted my lashes writing it on a random piece of paper I found.

She pulled up to my hotel and after saying see you later I walked to my room and threw myself on the bed dozing off immediately.

I groaned at the constant ringing my phone wouldn't stop making so I annoyedly pick up the phone not bothering to check who it was.

"Hey what's up? I thought you were going to call me" Sylvia spoke into the phone.

"I'm sorry I fell asleep" I sat up rubbing my eyes checking the clock next to me seeing it was almost 7pm.

ShitFace - Hey I'm at your hotel I'm coming up now.

I began freaking out trying to run around in a towel I just put on completely forgetting about Sylvia.

"Is everything okay why aren't you speaking?" Her face planted with concern and yes we're on FaceTime.

"Is it okay if I just call you tomorrow I'm kinda late for something."

"It's not like I haven't seen your body before, you could get dressed right here" she suggested running her tongue over her lips.

I began walking to the door as I heard a knock.

"Sylvia I have to go we'll speak another time I promise."

"Fine Iris, have fun. Don't forget about me sweetheart" she said in the middle of me opening the door.

Just as Sylvia said that I opened the door for Harley.

She cringed for some reason.

"Were you on the phone with someone?."

"Yeah sorry they just randomly called m-

"No it's okay, I just thought they sounded familiar" She nonchalantly answered sliding past me and making her way into the room.

Familiar?

Chapter 9

Iris POV

"Why aren't you ready Iris? I swear women take the longest to do everything" She scoffed sitting in the chair with a man spread.

"I told you I overslept shut it Harley" I buckled my heel strap standing up.

"Yeah well I've been sitting here for two hours" The woman threw her head back acting like a child.

I sprayed perfume and made sure I had everything I needed.

"You're so dramatic can't you see I'm ready" I rolled my eyes walking towards the door Harley not far behind me.

I felt eyes lurking behind me but ignored it.

If I were anyone else I'd check myself out too.

We decided to walk to the club instead of driving since we both would be drinking and so that I'd become familiar with the area.

We began walking and making slight conversation.

Somehow some way she got us into the club as soon as we got there instead of having to wait in the line that seemed to never end.

As soon as we were slipping through the crowd i was downing shots which thankfully loosened me up enough not to feel awkward.

Me and Harley were grinding on each other like we've known each other for years at a time.

Me rubbing my ass against her and her caressing my waist.

Usually I wouldn't let this happen, but why not?

It's friendly.

I then suddenly felt myself being pulled away from Harley and being shoved into another chest.

When I looked up it was the same woman from my first night clubbing.

"You didn't tell me you were coming and with someone else" She tilted her head.

I just looked at her with confusion and turned back to a annoyed Harley.

I placed my arm over her shoulder beginning to dance again— instead of being pulled away by Andi she kept trying to get my attention by tapping my shoulder or shouting my name over the music.

Harley's nostrils began to flare until she finally said something "Salope, je jure devant Dieu que si tu ne nous laisses pas tranquilles, je vais te trouver et—"

I tugged on her arm signaling she needs to stop doing whatever she's doing because she appeared to be upset.

The other woman just scoffed "Qu'est-ce qu'elle est ? Ta propriété."

"Laisse-moi deviner que la belle Iris ne t'avait pas dit que c'était moi qui la baisais, toute la nuit." She grinned.

Not a happy one either.

The one people use to cover their evilness— their true intentions.

I have zero clue what they were saying but I did know I was slightly intrigued by Harley's protectiveness and Andi's behavior.

I've only met the girl one damn time.

"Harley let's just go before you both cause a scene" I was dragging her away out the entrance taking a deep breath once we reached the atmosphere outside of the club.

We began walking back to my hotel in silence.

Her probably overthinking the situation and wondering why she did what she did.

Me wondering why she got so defensive over whatever they were talking about.

"She was talking about you, Iris. Did you fuck her?" She puffed her cheeks out.

I folded my arms as the breeze was beginning to pick up.

"We were drunk and I was horny. She initiated it though I don't understand why she acted the way she did but that was the first and last time. I hate possessive one night stands, I barely remembered her fucking name" I bit my lips.

Harley just hummed signaling she was attentive.

"Why do care so much anyways?" I asked the French woman out of curiosity as of to why she was so annoyed or stressed about the situation.

I don't care, Iris.

Chapter 10

Iris POV

And with that she walked off to her car leaving me in the middle of Paris alone.

I removed my heels as I was approaching the hotel. As soon as I got inside my room I took a quick shower and removed my makeup.

Mixed in-between if I should text Harley or not, I didn't. If she weren't to respond that would be humiliating so I just decided to call Sylvia before I slept.

Within the first three rings she picked up.

"What are you doing up so late Iris" Sylvia questioned but I knew she was smiling.

"I just came from an outing and it's pretty late there too so don't judge me" I fluffed my pillows and shut the blinds.

"I've missed you, your voice, your smile, your scent and the way you taste" She whispered the last part compelling me to bite my lips and take deep breaths.

"Don't you miss having me between your legs Iris? Me making them shake and you begging me to stop" Her accent was more present and my right hand wandered into my underwear as she began teasing me.

"Sylv—

"Don't interrupt me, you know you haven't been getting any Iris. Just sit back and let your fingers do the work while I talk to you sweetheart" I ran my finger up my slit feeling my juices and groaned at the frustration.

And let's just say we stayed on the phone for another hour.

Waking up at almost 1PM has to be the most irresponsible but most worth it think I've down out here so far.

Waking up to pure darkness because of the blackout curtains was a dream that came to an end all because of my stupid bladder.

After opening the curtains and deciding to stay in the room for today I ordered room service for breakfast and a typical breakfast.

I called my family checking in on them seeing if they needed any support and showed them my view from the balcony. It made my heart so warm that it felt like it was time for a quick trip back to my country.

When the 40 minute phone call was up I made a cappuccino and grabbed my laptop walking to the balcony and sat in the not so comfy chair.

Going over blueprints and what furniture and accessories the company I was working with would like in their lobby.

My phone began buzzing and I picked it up without checking who it was

A familiar French accent came about which triggered a sigh of irritation.

"What do you want Harley, I shouldn't even be speaking to you with the stunt you pulled last night leaving me there! And for a reason I don't know about" I scoffed.

"Stop being so stubborn and let me in, I'm already here."

I looked over the rail seeing a not so formal but comfortable dressed Harley who eventually walked inside the building to get to my room.

Within 5 minutes I heard a knock on the door and open it while assuring she saw my eye roll.

And of all the things to say she came up with.

"So, wanna scissor?"

Chapter 11

Harley POV

After I left her standing there I felt bad immediately. Not even I knew the reason as to why.

I felt annoyed by the bar girls presence, I especially got irked when I found out Iris was getting fucked by her and that was the reason as to why she was late to breakfast.

I'm only older because she was tardy. But then again I had no right to feel any type of way so that's exactly why I pushed everything behind me and drove to her hotel unexpectedly.

When I pulled up I saw her on the balcony looking intrigued and focused on her computer. But did that stop me from calling her?

Nope.

When she picked up she started bickering about last night. Which she had a reason to but sheesh I couldn't even talk.

"Stop being stubborn let me in, I'm already here" she scoffed and looked down from the balcony annoyance written all over her face but I knew it was just an act

After she left the balcony I made my way up quickly to her room door and knocked to which she answered pretty quickly.

My intrusive thoughts took over.

"So, wanna scissor?" I smirked knowing it would get to her but I was just joking.

Somewhat.

She was just about to close the door in my face but I shoved my way inside.

"Well that's no way to treat a lady now is it Iris."

"Oh please you would know about how to treat a lady with the shit you pulled last night pendeja" She glared at me as she moved past me to lock the door and sat on her bed with her chin on her knees.

"That's why I am here, to apologize and make it up to you someway" I took a deep breath and sat in front of her.

"That woman you obviously slept with just seems like bad news, especially the way she put her hands on you without a second thought. And you showed up late to breakfast because of her—

"Why do you care?" She interrupted me scrunching her eyebrows.

"I don't." I defensively responded getting a eye roll out of her.

"My point is that I'm sorry for leaving you there in the early morning hours because of the fact I got pissed off, and I hope this could be left behind us and we can move on and explore the city more until you go back home. If not I'll just go." I placed my cheek on my palm.

"It's fine it isn't that serious Harley, you could make it up to me by staying and watching a movie with me. I don't wanna leave my room today" Iris playfully pouted patting the spot next to her which was an indication I had no choice.

I scooted next to her and pulled the covers over our legs while hers were still up to her chest as she flicked through movies to watch.

As she finally came to one she found was watchable enough she looked up at me and we made short eye contact. She looked at me with a questionable look in her eyes.

Which were pretty big but in a cute way.

And rested her head on the my shoulder.

I felt stiff for a bit because i wasn't sure of what to do or if I should embrace her or not.

I wouldn't say she's a friend, i don't know what we are but I've never cuddled with a friend let alone anyone.

Finally pushing my thoughts aside I wrapped an arm around her waist from behind and brought her closer.

Within seconds we were relaxed in each other.

I could get used to this, I wouldn't mind staying like this for awhile.

Chapter 12

Iris POV

As I began to stir awake I felt movement under me, a chest moving up and down. It was quite calming but my bladder was being very alarming forcing me to get up and use the bathroom.

After using the bathroom and brushing my teeth I returned back to the room and ordered us room service for breakfast.

I don't know why it's hitting me we slept together.

It was fully clothed and innocent so is it really a big deal?

Checking my phone I received a hand full of messages from Sylvia.

Sylvia M. - It's so boring here without you.

Sylvia M. - I miss your moans and writhes under me.

Sylvia M. - I hope you're thinking of me.

Sylvia M. - Call me later.

I tossed my phone as soon as I read the last message.

It's something about her. I don't know what it is but I just can't find myself as interested in her as she is in me.

All I see is sex. Nothing more.

She's a good person but .. too clingy? Or maybe I just like the feeling of unacceptable women and not being able to have what I want do easily.

She's too easy.

I took a quick shower and as soon as I wrapped the towel around myself I heard a knock on the door indicating the room service was here.

I could tell the man was eyeing me but I chose to ignore it.

Just another perv in today's society.

We walked over to the bed and he pulled out a cart placing the breakfast on there neatly.

I gently shook Harley awake when the man left.

One eye opened and she tossed the covers over her face groaning and mumbling under her breath in French.

"No Harley get your ass up I didn't order all this food for nothing."

She sat up and bit her lips eyeing me "Are you on the menu too chérie?"

Her voice sounded very.. never mind.

I rolled my eyes grabbing an oversized shirt and shorts putting them on in the bathroom.

Harley still wasn't up when I returned from the bathroom so I decided to mess with her.

Climbing onto bed I stood up and balanced myself.

I placed my feet on both sides of her body and jumped on the bed jolting her awake almost immediately.

She looked up at me with annoyed and tired eyes.

Before I could stop myself from jumping on the bed I felt warm hands pulling me down onto her lap with a very secure grip.

Harley leaned closer causing me to shriek at the eye contact "Keep doing that and we'll be making this bed moving in all different directions, together." She gently squeezed my thighs.

After a few seconds of trying to get my breathing together I finally came to my senses.

I removed myself from her lap "Why are you like this, get up and get your morning breath together so we could eat or I'll just eat it all by myself."

Before getting up she stares at me with a look that was once again unbeknownst to me.

Her and her unreadable face.

When she was finished in the bathroom we ate and talked a bit more until she had to leave to do something for work since she put it off just so she could tour me.

I was getting bored and it was only noon here so I got dressed in a short fitted sun dress and bucket hat then made my way to a park with kids and animals and admired the area wishing Salvador looked this outside of the areas made for foreigners.

In my eyesight I caught a glimpse of a couple resting on the edge of a fountain and reading together as the girl rested between his legs smiling endlessly.

I sort of envied that and wished them nothing but happiness.

After taking in the scenery I wanted to take a picture but I had realized I left my phone in my room.

A break from my phone isn't so bad seeing as Sylvia is the only one who blows my phone up.

I walked across the street to the library viewing mostly books in French.

Just as I was about to reach to browse a book on the higher shelf i felt a figure brush against me from behind and the longer arm reached for the book.

I was a bit startled and turned around almost immediately.

Luckily it wasn't a stranger it was Harley.

But how'd she find me?

"Seriously you can't do that i could've punched you" i rolled my eyes snatching the book from her.

"Look I was worried and you weren't answering your phone so I had to make sure you were okay" she followed behind me like lost puppy but I could tell she was trying not to look over my body.

I looked back squinting my eyes at her "How'd you find me anyways."

She ran a hand through her hair with a slight grin she thought I didn't notice.

"You really think I wouldn't keep some type of tab on you to make sure you're okay and safe? What kind of friend do you think I am chérie?"

My heart dropped at the way she said friend.

"Most would find that weird but I guess it's thoughtful" I shrugged walking over to the register

"Oh and i meant to tell you"

You look good enough to eat Iris.

Chapter 13

Iris POV

I narrowed my eyes "Seriously what's up with you and your flirting" the cashier handed me my book and I thanked him walking out of the door with Harley not far behind me.

"So, you gonna tell me how you found me or?" I rhetorically asked knowing she wouldn't but it wouldn't hurt to ask.

"Nope. But we're going back to my place for the night, no questions asked. I made us reservations for tomorrow and we need to not be late because of your mischievous actions" She led us to her car opening the door for me and I muttered a thank you.

"Trust and believe I wouldn't have if I knew she was such an ass" I buckled my seatbelt rolling my eyes.

Harley drove off without saying anything but her finger was repeatedly tapping on the steering wheel.

It began to annoy me so I gently placed my hand over her active finger causing her actions to come to a halt almost immediately.

"Are you okay? It's obviously something on your mind and I think you should get it off of your chest one way or another. Whether it's speaking to me or you needing alone time" I softly spoke caressing the top of her hand.

"You're right. One way or another." She bluntly spoke.

When we reached her home she led me back to the room I was in before and grabbed me a large enough shirt and new underwear.

I don't know what's up with that girl and her mood swings but I hope whatever it is gets resolved because I hate to see her act like this even if I just met her I care.

Only because I'm a good person.

After my 45 minute shower consisting of me just standing in the water and reminiscing about my life I got out and dressed, my stomach wasn't about to hold off any longer and I needed to eat so I lured my way into the kitchen a bit anxious about her thinking I'd be snooping.

As I opened the fridge door I could've sworn I heard a squeak so I closed it and opened it again deep down knowing the door didn't make that noise but I chose to ignore the thought of another person in her bedroom.

That's disgusting.

I pulled out some milk and a bowl.

As I reached on my tip toes for the cereal a photo fell from a shelf as if it was meant to be hidden or left there on accident.

Just as I was about to flip it over to look at it I heard a loud moan from Harley's bedroom that definitely didn't belong to her, it shook me out of my curious daze and I hurriedly put the photo back on top of the fridge before pouring my cereal and hurried to the room I was in before I had to hear anymore.

After eating in silence i decided to call Sylvia to distract myself before I slept so she wouldn't bother me for the next few days.

And yes I've noticed the pattern of her not bothering me until a few days after I speak to her.

This time I FaceTimed her and she picked up pretty quickly.

"Yes Iris?" The woman back at home casually answered.

"Oh so that's how we're answering now Sylvia?" I sat my phone up on a pillow so she could see my upper torso and face along with the background.

Her eyes squinted as if she was looking for something behind me.

"Sylvia you okay?"

"Where are you?" I was taken back at her ignoring my comments.

"At a friend's apartment I met on the flight here. Why? What's wrong?" I questioned quite confused.

"Nothing it just.. it looks familiar I guess. Anyway I have something to tell you and I think you'll like it" She smirked but her surprises aren't something I usually enjoy.

"Oh god what is it Sylvia—

"I'm coming to Paris and I'll be there within the next twenty-four hours" She cut me off.

I was in utter shock and speechless.

This wasn't a surprise

This was a fucking nightmare.

Chapter 14

Iris POV

I was in the middle of an amazing dream when I heard the disruption of pots and pans being clashed together in the room.

Me trying to sleep through it wasn't going to happen so my eyes lazily opened and there was no other than Harley hovering over me banging the pans and pots together purposely over me.

"Who the fuck still wakes up early after having hours and hours of loud sex while they scolded me for doing the same thing" I rhetorically asked and pushed past her muttering the word dick and ensured she heard it.

I went into the bathroom and heard Harley shout to dress nice before exiting the room. I used the toothbrush I'm surprised she kept from the last time I was here.

And since we came straight from the book store to her apartment I had no clothes but I was still shocked to see dress options laid out on the bed.

I decided to pick the short red and fitted dress since I personally thought red contrasted perfectly against my skin and hair.

I couldn't do much with my hair since mine is straight and Harley's is curly so I just straightened it more than it already was.

Ignoring Harley was pretty fun to see especially when she'd say something and I'd look directly at her as I'd continue doing whatever I was doing.

The only time I broke silence was to ask when we were leaving but I still didn't know where she'd made us reservations to.

It came over me to stop being such bitch and to be more grateful but hypocritical people irk my soul but I also didn't plan on really communicating with her outside of France.

When we finally left it was about an hour until sunset and the drive to wherever we were going was silent so I decided to break it.

"I was pissed at you for scolding me the first day about being late for fucking just for you to around and fuck someone else when you forced me to go back to your place. And you still woke up earlier than me somehow. They must I've been mediocre." I muttered all in one breath trying not to think to hardly about what occurred in her bedroom last night.

"I woke up on time so why exactly are you upset again?" She perked her eyebrow with a sneaky grin.

"Never mind , where are we going?" Harley rolled her eyes at my change of subject.

"You'll see chérie" Twenty minutes later we pulled up to a valet parking area and the worker took the keys and went off with the car.

We walked down a long hallway to the other side of the doors and two men opened it for us and the Eiffel Tower was just a few feet away from us.

The view was jaw dropping and the lights on the tower made the structure look even better.

"I wanted to take you somewhere most tourist love to come but instead I booked us a dinner inside, alone." Harley spoke in her accent softening it at the word alone.

"Aww look at you not being an ass to me for once in your life" I gave her a fake smile but overall I really love how extreme she went to do this for me.

We walked the few feet to the elevator of the Eiffel Tower. Harley entered first and placed her hand out for me to take.

I accepted her guidance and held onto her not surprisingly soft hand and stood next to her inside the elevator up the Eiffel Tower.

The view was definitely something. Scary but beautiful. The sunset creating a golden hue over the city just made everything better.

Not to mention Harley still hadn't let go of my hand but I chose to ignore my conscience for the night and to let the night flow.

When we reached the restaurant she guided me outside the elevator and we were eventually greeted by some guy dressed in a tux.

He led us to our table right in the middle with a candle and three drink options along with some dimmed lights.

The place had velvet curtains and a beautiful chandelier on the ceiling right above us.

Whoever was lucky enough to be born and raised in France has to be one of many of god's favorites.

It's a beautiful place.

I couldn't help but smile the whole time up until we got to our table.

Harley pulled the chair out for me and I just had to be a little bit of a smartass.

"Wow you're such a gentlewoman, didn't expect that out of you" I playfully commented.

As always she just chose to ignore it and walked to her seat.

"I'd be such a amazing girlfriend don't you think?" She had her mischievous on display.

"I guess.. why? Because of this? I mean yeah it's nice and thoughtful but not all girls like materialistic things. Affection and loyalty is just as meaningful" I shrugged and sipped on the glass of water infront of me.

The French woman pouted trying not to slouch in her seat "Way to ruin a moment Iris."

"Sorry sorry, where'd you say you worked again? Some of the things you buy are extraordinarily expensive." I questioned genuinely curious no regular person would be able to rent out a place like this especially at a reasonable price.

"I said I'm a realtor. And then some. But how's your family back home? Any pets? Friends back home? No? Okay. What would you like to do tomorrow?" She quickly tried to change the subject.

Weird.

Chapter 15

Iris POV

The dinner is actually going great. Harley told few of the many memories she had as a kid. The ones she enjoyed at least. But this one question had been lingering in the back of my mind lately.

And I had the urge to let it out.

"Harley." I cut her off in response she tilted her head indicating she wanted me to go on.

"Why do you always flirt with me and make those sexual remarks?" I curiously asked the French woman.

She took a sip of her now almost empty glass of wine "I'm just a flirt Iris it's nothing."

I kept silent and looked in her direction until she made eye contact with me. I gave her the 'tell the truth' look in which she sighed.

"Well, Iris. You intrigued me from the moment I met you. You're always so grumpy and never hesitate to say anything smart. And I like it. You're not easy, at all. I also adore that, I love the fact you know your worth. I actually like hanging out with you and I fucking hate people. But somehow. You're an exception to that and I would never do all of this, reservations and shit for a stranger" Harley grabbed my hand from across the table and caressed it.

"Basically all I'm saying is—

I had to cut her off. Again.

"I get it, I really do. I don't know what it feels like to like someone but maybe this is it? I've never been in anything serious or talked to anyone before but I wouldn't mind trying something different, especially after all you've done for me so far. We'll get to know each other more but slowly."

"Just know that you don't owe me anything." The French woman gave my hand a gentle squeeze.

I retreated my hand "Oh I know. You're still sleeping alone or what not, there are still some things I need to know about" I grabbed my glass of water and sipped on it.

"Yeah yeah, slowly. Right."

I only hummed and nodded.

Even though we live in two different countries, let alone continents. I decided not to let it cross my mind yet.

Who knows how serious we'll get anyway.

Sylvia fucking terrifies me.

She somehow found my hotel and budged her way in my room without a care in the world.

"What the fuck? When did you get here and how did you find me?" I questioned concerned.

"It wasn't exactly hard but aren't you happy to see me? I've missed you" Her eyes spoke volumes. She was horny. And almost backed me into the bed completely but I pushed pass her.

"Sylvia we seriously need to talk to clarify some things." I grabbed her forearm and gently pushed her into one of the cushioned chairs.

"We can't do this anymore. You can't do this anymore. I don't know why you're like this over me but it needs to stop." I was practically begging her.

"What are you talking about? Are you sick? You're speaking nonsense Iris" The older woman nervously laughed with her furrowed brows.

"I'm not trying to hurt your feelings I promise. I just can't lead you on when I don't feel the same. I interested in someone else Sylvia, I've met someone else."

I really felt bad. I know she's all alone and I was basically all she had but love and affection from the wrong person just doesn't feel right. I knew she was hurt but I can't keep faking it. I have Harley now and I like Harley enough not to waste her time.

Sylvia began gathering her things, getting prepared to leave the room but before she could do so I shouted "We can still be friends" but she just slammed the door mid-sentence.

I'm really going to need a stress reliever.

Sooner or later.

After all it's the next morning after Harley and I's dinner and I'm exhausted. Imagine having to wake up to that.

I decided to head back to bed before Harley would come pick me up for another outing.

She's really sweet.

My slumber lasted another 4 hours before my body started to ache from laying down too long.

I got ready for the day and decided to take a walk.

As I was strolling down the street I came upon a cafe and decided to stop in.

I just then remembered I don't speak French.

Harley would very much come in handy right now.

I was peeking up at the menu a bit confused and I think I looked pretty obvious and lost for a woman to come up to me and offer to help.

"You need help don't you. You're in one of the areas that hates translating. Anyways what would you like to order?" The random woman with light brown shoulder length hair rambled which caused me to smile.

"Thanks, I'd like an iced coffee preferably. Whatever you'd recommend" I politely replied.

Furthermore the lady ordered for me and offered to pay but I declined just wanting to leave and trying to avoid bumping into someone like Amelia? Alyssa? Who fucking knows.

Harley was weirdly enough in my room already when I arrived back at the hotel.

I didn't even give her a key.

But I've learned not to question her random pop ups.

Rolling my eyes I sat my coffee down "I'm not even going to ask the obvious question."

"Are you ready to go?" She stood up and walked over to me.

She wore a tucked blouse with sleeves rolled and trousers.

God I love women.

"Hell no do you see what I'm wearing. Give me a few minutes I'll be ready" Pushing pass her I entered the bathroom scrambling around.

"Yeah that's what you women always say" The French woman huffed throwing herself back into the chair.

I shouted back at her from the bathroom "Oh hush what should I wear? You never tell me where we're going."

"Wearing nothing would be great."

"Wait never mind scratch that everyone would see you" Harley mumbled.

"It'll be cold wear pants" She spoke loud enough so that I could hear her in the bathroom.

I put together an outfit consisting of fitted cuffed mom jeans and I picked a random graphic shirt to tuck into it along with a pair of shoes.

I pinned half of my hair with a clip and hurried out not liking the idea of having someone waiting for too long.

I gathered a few things and hurried out the door.

She held the door open for me grabbing my hand soon after which caused me to look at her questionably.

Harley met my eyes "What?"

"I've never held someone's hand before" She locked our fingers at the mention of that.

"Well I guess this is one of the many first you'll have with me chérie" She softly spoke.

I guess so.

Upon her opening the door of a truck she wasn't driving and us driving for a bit we held hand the entire time until we reached some place. The tinted windows made it difficult for me to make out what it was.

When the automobile came to a stop Harley rounded it and opened the door for me once more.

She lifted me up which resulted in a squeal to exit my mouth.

When i was finally able to make out my surroundings we were at a helicopter landing pad.

It felt like I was hallucinating.

She's done so much and I've done nothing for her.

I don't owe her anything but it would be nice to do something for her for once. I'll indefinitely make sure I do before I leave france.

"Harley what is this" I was damn near speechless.

Her face plaster with concern "Do you not like it? It gets better I swear."

I quickly reassured her "No no I love it I just don't want you to think this is what it takes to make me happy. I would've been fine with hanging out at my hotel or at your apartment with you. I just don't want you to think I'm using you or anything because I'm not I swear. Aslong as we're spending time together I'm happy no matter where we are."

"Oh. You're right, I'm sorry. I thought girls liked this" She looked defeated.

Chapter 16

Harley POV

Besides Iris telling me I don't have to go all out to impress her we're currently enjoying ourselves on the helicopter to Cannes France.

There's more to it but this is just how we get there.

I know she's wondering how I have so much money and can afford all of this.

But that shall not discussed, ever.

She was now resting her head on my shoulder as we were approaching the city.

As we were landing her eyelids were getting heavy.

I guess I could postpone our plans for later.

I thanked the pilot as he opened the helicopter door for us.

I gently shook Iris awake and exited the helicopter holding my hand out for her immediately after.

She shook her head tiredly "Carry me."

I immediately complied and scooped her up carrying her bridal style carefully as she rested her head on my shoulder with her arms around my neck.

"You don't get sea sick, do you?"

"Nope I haven't been in the sea to find out, where are we? Are we on a fucking boat?" Iris ecstatically moved out of my grip as she slowly turned around the whole boat realizing we were surrounded by water.

I walked up to her "I'm assuming your tiredness has vanished."

"I know how you feel about me being all extra and going all out with our outings but I will most likely never stop and you have way more to look forward to, so, do you like it?" Iris slowly faced me and after a few seconds jumped into my arms.

Her face was practically shoved in my boobs causing her to sound muffled "I love it , it's perfect."

"Then you'll be stoked about the inside" I grabbed her hand and guided her inside the yacht.

"There are three rooms. Ours is full sized with the others being half sized. The pilot and captain will be staying in those" I quickly explained as we walked pass the rooms of the captain and pilot.

Iris was still dumbfounded but made eye contact with me as I was speaking "Ours?" The Spanish woman questioned.

"Yes Iris, Ours."

After our exchange I showed the shorter woman the room we'd be staying in.

She damn near gasped at the sight as she slowly looked around the room.

She was obviously speechless which I found adorable.

"Wanna drive the boat?" Her face lit up at the question.

"Let me guess, you've never driven a boat before?" I knowingly questioned.

Iris grabbed my hand and dragged me away "Nope."

I knew she didn't know where she was going so I led the way to the cockpit guiding her inside.

"Alright I'm going to let you steer and sail a little bit away from the beach" I gently cupped her hands and placed them on the steering wheel guiding her hands with mine "Now turn it to the right."

Okay, I'm lying it's driving itself but she is doing a little something.

Ensuring the autopilot was on I guided her to the railing to take in the sunset and breeze of the water.

Iris held onto the railing while she looked overboard, her hair was flying all over the place.

I stepped behind her protectively as she was looking down.

"Question, what ever happened to those girls? You know, the one from the plane and the one you fucked the other day?" Iris's question caught me off guard but I took no time to answer her.

"That was a one time thing. I don't even remember her name to be honest."

Iris didn't turn around but still responded "So you get around?"

I forgot overthinking comes with liking a woman.

But it takes nothing to reassure them.

"I wouldn't be doing any of this if it wasn't just you in the picture."

Believe me.

Chapter 17

Iris POV

All these questions about her life wandered in my mind, especially questions about her love life.

We had just gotten ready for bed after we'd both finished taking our showers.

The shower was serene.

It gave me time to think, overthink. It gave me time to take in this new change in my life.

It's not like we're exclusive or in a relationship.

Just dating more or less testing the waters.

But that girl. The girl she had in her room the night before we went to the Eiffel Tower. The idea swarmed my mind. What if they were still talking and fucking around.

Even though she said it was nothing it still bothered me and I'd never hold back from speaking my mind.

Me overthinking won't help the situation, it'll only make me feel hostile towards her and I don't want to be that way towards someone who's not even mine but who does so much for me as a friend— or whatever we are.

"Harls, sit and brush my hair." I commanded as I handed her the vintage beige brush.

I sat on the ottoman facing the mirror as Harley stood behind me taking the brush gently brushing my wavy waist length hair.

We made eye contact through the mirror "What's up? Is everything okay" Worry occupied her face.

"Something's just been fogging my brain and I need—

Harley sighed "Iris if this is about the woman from the other night I still stand by what I said. I swear it's only you I want and am interested in. You're my only priority, the only one i will ever think about as long as you let me have you. You mean a lot to me even if we aren't together yet. I do want to make you mine and I will. But you'll have to trust me first, trust is one of the main things we need to help us get to where we want to be." I looked down fiddling with my fingers.

"I know but I'm still a very loyal person even in the beginning stages" and I'd hate to restrict myself from her by letting my mind take control but I'd also hate to give too much.

"So am I— how can you be so sure of something you've not given me the chance to show yet?"

She was right, I had no reason to doubt her. It's not like she did it while we were in the talking stage.

I need to trust her in order for this to work and I really want this to work. Without her who know what I'd be doing right now.

I'd probably already be back home messing around with Sylvia.

I've experienced many of my first with her and I want to continue stepping out of my comfort zone, stepping out of it with her makes everything feel worth and as more surreal than it already is.

And whatever we are— our situationship needs to take a step forward.

I know I said slow but come on.

It wouldn't hurt to get her mind going.

So I decided to do something I never thought I would ever initiate first.

I stood up from the ottoman and swiftly turnt around towards Harley.

I looked up at her puzzled face as I took the brush from her and sat it on the dresser.

I wrapped my left arm around her shoulder tangling her hair in between my fingers and slowly pulled her closer to me but stopped to look into her eyes to confirm it was okay with her.

As soon as I got permission I gently pressed my lips onto hers taking in the feeling of her lips for the first time.

And let me tell you-

They're the softest and sweetest thing I've ever had my lips against.

Harley's way with me was tender but carful.

I could tell she was holding back and was being respectful.

I fucking love that.

"Focus Iris" she reconnected our lips once more.

After a few moments Harley slowly slid her sleek tongue into my mouth getting a feel of every crevice in my mouth.

As if she was familiarizing herself with it.

Within minutes it was getting hotter and heated.

The things on the dresser were getting aggressively pushed aside and I was getting lifted onto the dresser with Harley in between my bare thighs hungrily attacking my lips but I knew how to keep up with her.

For now at least.

Her hands were starting to itch their way up my thigh.

I placed my palm on top of her hand and pulled away.

"Not yet" I muttered onto her lips sliding off the dresser grabbing onto her soft slender hand leading her to the king sized bed that stood in the middle of the room.

Just because I planned on making her wait and was talking things slowly didn't mean we couldn't make out and tease each other.

When we reached the bed I pushed her onto it and straddled her immediately after, grabbing her face which made her have duck lips. I slightly chucked pressing our lips together.

This went on for awhile before we finally decided to rest for our plans for tomorrow.

We were planning on going to the beach and I was curious to see if she'd behave differently now that things have changed.

Harley fell asleep with her arm protectively over my torso.

We were close enough as to where I could feel her body heat and hear her steady heartbeat but we weren't close enough to call it cuddling.

Ever since I've met her my life's changed tremendously and for the better.

She's become the highlight of my day— something I look forward to.

The sunshine who brings the Iris I want to be or not the Iris who's alone and annoyed with everyone.

And regardless of everything that's happened so far throughout the trip.

I wouldn't trade this for anything.

Chapter 18

Iris POV

Me and Harley were getting ready to leave the boat dock as we approached the beach.

I wore a very revealing solid white bikini with sunglasses sitting on top of my head.

Harley didn't seem like the type to get mad about what you wore, just about the sexualization or if I felt uncomfortable.

I really liked that about her but hell I like everything about her.

We grabbed our towels and sunscreen which Harley insisted on carrying.

Harley carried three towels, a bottle of sunscreen and a bag of snacks that was ridiculously heavy with her right arm causing her muscles to flex as her left hand occupied mine.

We walked down the slippery yacht stairs hand in hand down the dock to the fairly populated beach.

Ever since last night Harley had been very consistent with her kisses, it was like I received one every other minute but

I'm not complaining it's a step further from where we were before.

After we picked our spot and sat our towels down on the sand I handed Harley the bottle of sunscreen and laid on my stomach "Mind putting some on for me?" I knew she'd do it but I just wanted to see her self control with how revealing my bikini was, not that I was teasing her..

"Of course" She nodded squirting some onto her palm slightly rubbing it together "Where exactly do you need it Iris?" The French woman bit her lip.

I turned my head the other way as I began to smirk knowing I'd get to her "Wherever your hands take you cariño" i purposely wiggled my ass towards her in anticipation.

She finally began applying it in a massaging manner.

She started with my shoulders then her hands cautiously itched down my back and she was obviously trying to avoid my ass.

I decided to push it "Don't be shy, I don't mind. You wouldn't want me having a sunburnt ass now would you Harley?" I teasingly questioned.

She hovered over me her breath tickling the nape of my neck "The cause of your ass being red can be demonstrated in many other ways I'm willing to show you. Sooner or later atleast" She smirked before kissing my cheek and tending back to the sunscreen.

Oh? She wants to play that game.

I only grinned knowing she was waiting on me to be ready but that didn't mean we couldn't tease.

"I think that guy over there likes what he sees."

Harley looked to her left to catching a older man indeed eyeing her hand placement which was no more than a few centimeters away from my ass.

She glared at him and flipped me onto my back.

My lips were in between hers in no time.

With her knee right in between my legs not close enough to press itself against me but close enough for me to graze against it and get a sound out of me.

I lifted my neck and rested on my palms.

Her hand now rested behind my neck and played with the hairs behind it as she sucked and nibbled on my bottom lip.

She pulled away after a few more pecks and stared into my eyes "Have I ever told you how possessive I can get Iris?"

"And have I ever told you how much it turned me on?" I caressed her ivory by cheek.

I wanted to continue this but we had just gotten here and I didn't want to leave so soon so we ran into the water hand in hand.

Every so often she'd trick me into thinking she'd want something and would submerge me in water playfully but not without make sure she has a could grip on me even though I could swim.

I'd never laughed or smiled this much before let alone before her.

I always kept a resting face which apparently didn't look very inviting but the annoying woman I met on the plane was bringing a side out of me I wish I'd discovered years before and I wouldn't have it any other way.

A hour later we decided to go back to the boat to shower and play a few board and card games.

We eventually had dinner and laid in bed cuddled up enjoying our last night in Cannes on this yacht.

Now I could add being on a yacht to my checklist of things I've never experienced before, before the French woman who made me undeniably happy.

We'd be heading back to Paris tomorrow and I'm anxious to see what she has planned for us to do next.

I always enjoy myself with Harley.

Which meant I was dreading having to go back home.

She makes me want to live here, in France, with her.

Chapter 19

Iris POV

"Bonjour chérie" I was awakened by Harley's raspy voice and a kiss on the cheek as my ass was pressed against her.

I was kind of sad about leaving this place but with Harley being Harley I knew I had more to look forward to.

I only groaned turning over snuggling my face into her neck "Just a bit longer" I mumbled.

"Well, while I let you rest a bit longer I'll go check to see if breakfast is ready" She finally got up leaving the room.

After a few moments of not being able to fall back asleep I got up and took a quick shower and got ready for the day.

I wandered the yacht looking for Harley but stumbled upon the railing at the head of the yacht overlooking the water.

The boat was moving at a decent speed but speedy enough to have my hair flying everywhere.

I suddenly felt a presence behind me, arms wrapping around my waist causing me to jump.

I gasped quickly turning around "Shit Harley don't do that what if I fell overboard" I glared at her holding my chest where my heart was.

"I'm sorry, I couldn't help but to admire you while you were in your own little world but I just came to tell you that breakfast is ready. Whenever you're ready" She softly spoke walking away after I nodded.

"I'll be there in a bit" I called after her.

I haven't used my phone since I've been here I wonder if Sylvia contacted me.

Things have been too perfect plus I was due for a visit in El Salvador.

I needed to visit my family but I'd ponder about that later.

I stepped away from the railing making my way to breakfast with Harley.

We spent about a hour and a half eating and talking about random stuff until it was time to leave.

"So your place or mine?" Harley's eyes peeked no lower than my neck while my tank made my chest appear more plump and cleavage more revealing.

I shrugged "Well, I was thinking about maybe going back to my hotel to get my things then going back to yours? Not like I'm even there anyway, no point in paying for it."

"Alright, we'll stop there as soon as we land." She nodded as she helped me inside the helicopter and placed the earphones onto my head.

That's another thing I like about her; she finds the littlest reasons and ways to help me with things without me having to ask.

Even though I'm all about having my independence, I enjoy her and her little successful attempts at being a gentlewoman.

It makes me realize how she hasn't mentioned her family seeing as she knows how to treat people as if she was raised in a home you'd speak highly of.

But hey I can't assume what her childhood was like based on how she treats people now. She could've came from shit but I'm better off asking considering she has yet to tell me and I'm curious.

I decided to ask when we were in the air a good amount of time and when everything was smooth and steady.

Her lips I've inevitably tasted caught in between her teeth as her long dark lashes lightly brushed against her cheekbone as her eyes were lowered.

I've noticed she'd do it when something was either bothering her or she was in deep thought.

I gently placed my palm on top of hers "What's on your mind?" I softly asked the French woman ensuring I was listening by keeping eye contact.

"Nothing. Just.. reiterating my life" She half grinned.

I began caressing her hand with my thumb as a sign of support "Wanna talk about it?"

"It's nothing. I was just thinking about how it'll be when you have to go back home. It'll be so fucking boring and lonely."

"But I also have you to look forward to. And you make up for any ounce of aloneness I've ever felt. You fill in that gap. I like having you around and I know it'll be hard when you do decide to go back home" She sighed.

"We don't have to think about that right now. I'm not leaving anytime soon we still have things to learn and experience together. Let's just enjoy each other's presence and company while we can." Harley's pouty face made it clear she'd understood.

I leaned in and gave her a few quick pecks and pulled away.

Maybe now was a good time to ask about her parents.

"Do you wanna talk about them? Your parents, how are they?" I spoke hoping I made it obvious she didn't have to answer.

But she did.

"I was a result of a first time mistake. Dad knocked my mom up. Typical high schoolers. She had me her junior year, she's 43 now. She actually likes women which is why she barely liked my dad around. The thought of her being intimate with him made her disgusted. But hey what can I say we have that in common. I talk to my dad occasionally they co-parented up until he got into some shit and my mom cut him off for good and I have a pretty decent relationship with him regardless of what he does and that he can rarely talk. My mom on the other hand.."

She sighed dragging her hand over her face.

"— She a totally different story for a different time. I can barely stand to be around her it's why she moved away to America. I hate her so much I drove her to move away."

Harley took my chin in between her thumb and index finger pulling me in.

"Now it's just about you and me. Okay?"

She was only a slight brush away from letting our lips meet.

But she decided to be a ass and moved back into her seat with a smirk on her face.

I glared at her "Tease."

I put my AirPods in under the protective earphones for the rest of the time we had left in the helicopter.

Believe it or not I've been listening to French music my whole time here just so I could feel apart of the community even if I didn't understand a single thing they were saying.

At least the tempo was nice.

When we landed it was still pretty early— About noon.

Harley being the typical sweetheart she was helped me out of the helicopter and opened my door to the designated truck that was always here to get us if she didn't want to drive.

This girl has got to be rich what ordinary person just randomly has a driver to take them wherever they want.

But whether she was rich or not it didn't matter, I would still be happy as shit enjoying our little adventures together and the memories we made.

We were currently in the elevator up to my hotel room to get my belongings to take back to her place so it would be more convenient and we'd be able to see each other more.

The elevator moved pretty slow so I'm guessing Harley took it as a good sign to push me against the wall of the elevator initiating a make out session.

My legs wrapped around her and those three minutes seems to go buy pretty slowly.

Probably because my hand was wandering and pressing random floor numbers and we definitely didn't stop when we heard the doors ding.

When it began to get hot she pulled away tugging on my bottom lip.

"We'll hopefully finish this later" Her thumb wiped under my now pink lips.

We pressed the right floor my room was on and actually waited this time.

Walking up to my room number I pulled out the room key.

Just before I could hover the key over the padlock my room door opened causing my heart to drop to my ass.

The lack of privacy didn't scare me.

It was the person behind the door who did.

My brows immediately furrowing at them.

My tone getting ready to sound snarky.

"Sylvia?"

Harley's jaw gaped in disbelief.

"Mom?"

Chapter 20

Harley POV

This cannot be happening again.

"How do you know her Iris?" I sighed as I questioned her with my hands dragging ,over my face.

We were back at my apartment now.

Iris refused to talked to her so I spoke to my mother privately while Iris was getting her things from her room.

We agreed to meet tomorrow to talk possibly for the last time.

"I met her in a grocery store back in Texas. It's all starting to make sense now, she mentioned having a daughter who didn't like her but I never really payed it any mind I just wanted the one thing from her I knew she was willing to give me" She mumbled seemingly ashamed.

I rolled my eyes seeing as I was used to it "Let me guess, she fucked you?"

Iris barely nodded.

"I'm so sorry" She said in a shaky voice.

"Don't be. It isn't the first time Iris" I stood up.

Her lips parted in "What?"

I might as well give her the backstory.

"When I came out m my mom of course supported me since she realized she also liked women soon after. My luck at relationships failed dramatically in high school because of her. Senior year before I was 18 I got emancipated from her. Any other person would call it a first love but I'd call it a dodged bullet. I began talking to a girl who was very quiet and to herself. I made it my priority to talk to her and be her friend. After a handful of months of getting to know her and breaking her out of her shell we began dating. She was already 18 before me. I brought her home to meet my mom better known as Sylvia for her birthday dinner. My mother insisted on me going to pick up dinner—

"When I came back half an hour later i assumed they didn't hear me coming through the door" I huffed recalling the rush of events my teenage years brought me.

Iris made from eye contact with me the whole time without any interruptions so I continued.

"I found them on the couch together.. her head between my girlfriend legs."

Start flashback.

Are my eyes playing tricks on me or is my mother seriously doing this to me again.

"Mère I can't fucking believe you! You said you wouldn't do this shit anymore" I screamed at her as they shuffled from the couch.

"Get the hell out of my house Camille" I gritted with my fist balled trying to suppress my anger.

She sprinted out of the door but not before trying to apologize.

When she was finally out of the door I could tell the woman I was about to disown as my mother was getting prepared for me to yell at her.

Ever since I caught her the last two times either kissing, touching or having sex with the girls I've talked to or she knew I liked she swore she'd never do it again since our relationship meant more to her than a girl but that went down the drain today.

"Fille it just happened she came onto me" The woman I once looked up to lied.

"Doesn't matter. I'm getting emancipated I can't deal with this anymore. You're a horrible mother."

"You make me never want to give love a try ever again" I spoke through my teeth feeling my nose burning and vision blurring.

I don't cry.

Within two months I was already learning to be independent on my own and a adult.

With my own apartment my father gifted me it made things easier.

I've been giving my mother the cold shoulder as well as Camille.

If this is how it's going to be every time I want to pursue a girl.. I won't pursue anyone ever again.

- End flashback.

By now Iris's palm was on my cheek trying to comfort me while I told her the mini backstory.

"I swear I didn't know. She somehow found my hotel a few days ago and I told her off and that I would no longer pursue it because of you. Because I want you instead. I never felt anything for her I knew the person for me was somewhere out there and that person just turned out to be her daughter" She reassured.

My stubbornness made it difficult for me to believe her but i felt as if I knew her well enough to know she wouldn't do that purposely.

It's not the fact she slept with someone else— I didn't even know her at the time but it's the fact it's my mom.

Who I hate so very much—

Got to have Iris first; the first woman I've allowed to be more than just a hookup since my teen years because she deserves more then that just as well as I do.

But Sylvia didn't know of Iris either.

Iris didn't owe me loyalty then, Sylvia doesn't owe me loyalty now.

"I'm not mad at you." I rubbed my cheek against her warm palm.

"Good cause' even if you were I wasn't going anywhere" She leaned on her tip toes giving me a quick kiss before pulling away.

My hands reached the back of her neck "It'll be a bit weird but this doesn't change anything for me. Only because it's you and because I really like you. Yeah the situation is fucked up but you mean more to me than she ever has and I won't let her ruin the one thing that makes me happy anymore. I promise."

"You mean so much to me too. She never had a chance at getting me let alone taking me away from you. I'm all yours. I'll give you as much space and time as you need okay? Just tell me" My spanish girl wrapped her shorter arms around me engulfing me in a tight hug.

I know what I need to do.

It's now currently the next day. Noon.

I made sure to feed Iris before leaving to meet Sylvia at the local park.

Iris has been acting a bit giddy and been more touchy.

Dragging her hands down my back or wrapping her thighs around me grazing her hands purposely over my tits or ass.

Not that I particularly minded but I'm going to eventually have hard time controlling myself.

It's already hard enough since I see her everyday.

But that's not the point.

I was now walking up to the picnic table she was sitting at.

That's one thing about her. She's never late. Ever.

Probably the only thing I've inherited from her.

"To save both of us time I'm going to make the shit short and sweet mère" I glared at her as I sat down.

"Good evening to you too fille" She smile as if she wasn't phased by any of this.

"I want you out of here. Out of me and Iris's life for good. You've already caused enough trouble, she doesn't want you here and I sure as hell don't. And when I say I want you out of here I mean forever. I don't even want to see you in public. Move to a different country.. do something just leave us alone we were happy before you came and we'll continue to be happy whether you like it or not. So, what will it take for you to comply?" I made it as simple as I could with my hands folded neatly in front of me as I managed to suppress my anger.

I thought I saw some sort of regret on her face but I didn't care enough to pay it anymore mind to it than I already had.

Sylvia sighed grabbing her purse and stood up tall hovering over me.

She smirked "It won't take anything. I'll go. Make her happy, she deserves it."

"I'm sending you both my best regards. I love you Harley. Goodbye Harley."

And with that she disappeared amongst the many strangers. Forever.

Atleast for now.

I know better then to believe anything that comes of her mouth.

I went home to Iris after sitting there feeling the temporary relief wash over me.

When I walked through the door she was playing with my cat—

Esme.

Tickling and holding her paws caressing her fur.

She didn't even realize I was back.

"Well aren't you two cute" I smirked walking up to them.

I haven't been spending as much time as I should with my cat especially with my schedule but that changed after Iris and I spent a few minutes playing with the cat and feeding her treats.

Iris bit her lip as she faced me "I'm going to the pool and you are too" She started walking towards the bathroom in my bedroom as she removed her shirt halfway there looking back at me with a smirk leaving me wondering what my eyes were missing out on.

I went into the other bathroom rinsing myself before changing into a bathing suit top and matching shorts — casual enough for me.

When I came out Iris dragged me to the pool built into the roof of my apartment.

This time she wore a baby blue bikini that looked amazing on her.

Everything looked amazing on her.

As soon as we reached the pool she slid in and I followed suit trying not to stare at her ass.

She lowered herself into the water her neck and head the only thing out of the water.

She had some type of seductive look on her face as her hair was slicked back and she had specks of water on her pinkish-redish lips caught in between her teeth.

She's a fucking siren.

Iris tilted her head to the left "Why don't you come here cariño?"

Her sultry voice called out to me immediately causing me to be only a few inches away from her in no time.

Her hands met my waist and she unexpectedly pushed me up against the wall of the pool.

It didn't hurt but the force was notable causing my body to grow hot.

I hummed leaning down inches away from her lips "Mmm my strong girl, is this what you like? Pushing me against the wall" Iris nodded as her hands traveled further down towards the bands of my swim shorts.

I gently grabbed her wrist pulling them out of the water and flipped us around pushing her up against the wall instead "Too bad chérie."

With her hands tangled in my wavy hair she tugged down on my neck pulling me where I knew she wanted me.

"That's my job" I whimpered against her lips finally allowing them to meet.

Iris's arms were wrapping themselves around my shoulders as she became more needy during our kiss shoving her tongue inside my mouth.

My hands were traveling up and down her waist resisting the urge to grab her ass.

I swiftly lifted her and she wrapped her legs around my waist pulling us closer to each other.

Iris was beginning to moan into the kiss causing me to get even more aroused than I already was.

She pulled away leaning our foreheads against each other.

"Let's go back to your room" She softly spoke guiding us out of the pool.

I wasn't sure what was happening but she was acting like a succubus and not like her usual passive serene annoyed with the world self.

When we reached my room Iris's grip on my waist tightened as we got approached my bed.

She flipped us so I was now in front of her with my back facing the bed.

Within seconds Iris pushed me onto the bed climbing on top of me; straddling me with her locs of long wet hair covering some of her face as she hovered over me.

Is she going to fuck me?

Chapter 21

Harley POV

No. I'm doing the fucking.

I flipped the smaller woman over as she began kissing down my neck. I couldn't continue doing anything until i was 100% sure she wanted to move forward with it.

"Are you sure you wanna do this? There's really no rush Iris" I asked as i hovered over her.

She nodded eagerly pulling me down to her lips by the nape of my neck.

Not wanting to move too fast i parted her thighs gingerly and pressed my thigh against her clit inciting a moan out of her.

Iris pulled the string of my bikini top and ran her hands down my shorts and over my ass "I know you want to move slow but not at a damn snails pace Harley" She then cupped my pussy making me gasp.

I had no idea she was like this in bed.

She ran her fingers through my folds causing my thigh to press further into her.

"Fuck stop teasing already" Iris moaned in my mouth.

I guess i could speed this up a bit.

After swiftly pulling her bikini bottoms the side and thoroughly spreading her wetness I plunged two fingers inside of her immediately after sensually thrusting.

Not too fast nor too slow.

Her back arched off the bed as our lips were aggressively pressed closer.

Iris moved her head to the side, her nose shoved in my curly hair as her moans were directly hitting my ear.

Her moans were a mental indicator to go faster so I did.

Moans and wet sounds echoed across the room as my fingers constantly pumped inside her pussy.

"More Harley" Iris stuttered between moans.

I peppered a few kisses on her face before dragging them down her neck and collarbone dragging my wet tongue down her cleavage capturing a nipple in between my teeth through the cloth.

I tugged the intruding cloth down her torso accidentally ripping it causing Iris to glare at me.

"It was cheap. I'll buy you a new one" I shrugged.

And here it was, my first view of her breast. It almost felt like a reward, like I should cherish it.

And I was.

Capturing a bare nipple between my teeth and the other between my free hand I slowed down the pace of my finger inside her dripping pussy harshly sucking at her nipple and pinching the other.

Iris adjusted my head to look up at her "Let's move to the shower."

I swiftly picked the smaller woman up drawing my attention right back to her breast.

I turned the water and removed all my clothing shortly entering the shower and holding Iris up against the wall.

I circled my thumb around her slippery clit again removing my mouth from her nipples but to her neck suctioning the flesh.

"Fuck baby don't stop" she loudly whimpered pushing herself against my practically wet palm.

I groaned at the sound of her moans and wetness.

I halted and carefully placed Iris down as I bent and began dragging my tongue down her stomach and sucking creating hickeys all the way down from her neck to her inner thighs.

Avoiding the star of the show I continued sucking her bruised flesh.

I was finally face to face with the one thing I was going the cherish every moment with while I had it. Lowering my head between her thighs after harshly separating them more and placing them on my shoulder so I could see her fully I eagerly began eating at her.

My tongue glided in between her slit from her opening to her clit her sweet taste getting me immediately addicted.

"Oh my- fuck yes" Iris's hand flew to my hair pulling me closer her hips meeting my tongue expertly.

I re-entered my fingers inside her soaking entrance eagerly thrusting as my tongue repeatedly flicked against her throbbing clit.

"Don't stop" the woman above me spoke just as her walls were becoming tighter indicating hr comes.

Her moans could probably be heard throughout my whole apartment but who cares she needs this and I've been yearning to taste her—

To please her.

I sped up the pace of my fingers creating more friction just as I began sucking on her pulsating clit.

"I'm so close don't stop" She cried out.

I wouldn't dare stop until she's finished.

After a few more thrust into her pussy she came undone screaming my name.

I slurped her clean running my tongue through her folds a few more times just as she calmed down from her first climax of the night.

"You look so beautiful after you've been fucked chérie" I muttered as I kissed up her body clashing our lips as soon as I made it up to her jaw.

"That was the best sex; orgas I've ever gotten Harls" the breathless girl spoke as I hovered over her.

"Oh I hope you don't think we're done sweetheart, we're far from it" I smirked.

I began nibbling her earlobe "But there is something I wanted to ask you" I seductively whispered into the flustered girls ear.

Iris groaned "What is it?"

"Be my girlfriend?"

I woke up to the other side of the bed where Iris slept empty.

Cliché.

I got up to brush my teeth and wash my face but even then she wasn't back.

But before I could complain the shorter girl came walking in with my shirt barely covering her thighs and her dark wavy hair resting at her waist with her phone in her hand.

Thoughts of the many orgasms I gave her till' the early hours of the morning resurfaced.

"Buenos dias novia" My favorite voice spoke as she made her way towards me.

"What?"

Iris gave a teasing smile "I said, Good morning girlfriend."

I could only smile and be happy that she's somewhat mine, I'd never ask anyone to be my girlfriend in the middle of sex but now this just gives me a reason to be as jealous as I wanted while also letting my intrusive thoughts win until I have her officially but I'll let that be a surprise.

"Good morning beautiful, why are you up so early? You never are , especially willing" I grabbed a pillow shoving my face in it.

"I didn't say attack me asshole" I felt her hard glare through the pillow.

"Anyways I did something while you were asleep and it would typically be too soon to do this but no offense I'm so fucking tired of mean the French people who get mad I don't understand what the hell they're sayingI like what the fuck

Anyways I've been getting a taste of your country so I think it's time you get a taste of mine" I heard her sigh after she realized she was rambling.

She's so fucking cute.

"I got us tickets to El Salvador to see my family."

Just then I threw the pillow across the room which by the way almost hit Iris in the head I gained me a hard stare in return.

"Sorry Sorry. You did what exactly?" I nervously laughed scratching the back of my head.

"Not so tough now are you?" She evilly smirked.

Be ready by 9pm tomorrow night.

Chapter 22

Iris POV

I was about half asleep before I felt a pair of wandering hands against my torso as my back was turned away from them with my ass pressed against their lower torso.

The hands I obviously knew belonged to my girlfriend slid themselves up my breast and cupped them causing me to bite my lower lip as I pretend to still be asleep.

Her hands lowered themselves again but this time to the hem of my shorts. The warm hands entered themselves inside my shorts meeting the bare skin underneath. I felt her head pressed against my shoulder her breath fanning my ear "I know you're awake baby but since you wanna be that way" She spoke peppered soft kisses against my shoulder and up my neck to my ear "Why don't I wake you up my way?" And just like that her fingers were deep inside me immediately jolting my eyes open as a throaty moan left my lips.

Then she fucking stopped "See how easy that was?" She leaned over quickly kissing my lips as she removed her fingers and placed them in her mouth licking her lips after "I have a quick meeting online I'll be in the other room" I was still in shock as she was walking towards the bathroom. Who the fuck does that?

I sat up and checked the time on my phone it was only 11am and I had plenty of time to sleep in but she just wanted to be an asshole especially with that shit she just pulled.

I got up a few minutes later after she was finished in the bathroom and got myself ready for the day. While in the shower I came up with a perfect way of getting her back, I just hope she can be quiet, for her own sake atleast.

I finished up and dressed in some simple mom jeans and a cropped shirt then tied my hair so it wouldn't be in the way of what I was about to do.

Sometimes I don't feel 24.

I quietly made my way to the other room Harley was in and peeked my head in but she was too busy talking to notice me while her laptop sat in front of her, she was wearing a simple white blouse with a few buttons undone her cleavage on show for whoever was in that meeting but her hair which was wet and damped the area of her breast— covered it a bit. She hadn't noticed me yet and just hearing her speak french turned me on even more.

God she's so fucking hot.

I got down on my knees and crawled under her desk as fast as I could without being noticed.

By the time I was completely under the desk and in front of her legs she was still talking but I truly didn't care. I placed my palms on her thighs and brought them higher up her body.

She didn't even flinch when I touched her and continued talking. Harley lowered her gaze to where my hands were on her toned stomach and averted her eyes to mine furrowing her brow in the sexiest way possible without even trying.

She finished speaking then went on mute "The hell are you doing?" She carelessly slouched.

"Finishing what you started. Hope you can keep quiet, that man seems to be very serious" i fluttered my lashes pointing to wherever the laptop was.

Harley smirked "Have at it" then took herself off of mute.

Is she serious? It's like she's doubting my abilities to please her.

I unzipped her trousers aggressively tugging them down causing her to glare at me as she slightly lifted her hips.

"Get a grip you tore my bikini" I muttered shoving her underwear down.

On second thought I changed my mind. I want to hear her.

There it was. Right in front of me, and all I need to do is lean in, and have my very first taste of her.

But why not drag it on a little more? Make her want it.

She wants to be petty I'll be petty right back.

I slowly caressed her thighs planting kisses I knew she could barely feel, I drug my nails down her thighs to her knees hearing her wince at the slight pain, I began parting her legs further apart giving me the best view of her. I stuck my finger in my mouth wetting it then glided it from her opening to her clit tracing faint circles around the aching bud.

I looked up to see her opening and closing her fist, her nails digging into her palm. I leaned forward faintly planting kisses around her clit purposely sticking my tongue out, her other hand tightly gripped the armrest as my tongue fully came down on her clit slowly flicking while my finger still rubbed at her opening debating on entering or not.

I assumed it was her turn to speak so I did what any sane person would.

I flicked faster running my palms over her toned stomach under her blouse carelessly dragging my nails against her belly.

She winced again but cleared her throat and continued talking.

I didn't like that.

I captured her clit between my lips and began urgently sucking and tugging purposely making slapping sounds every time I let the bud go.

In the middle of her sentence her words sounded jumbled and rushed as she tried to control her moaning but that just encouraged me more.

Her thighs were beginning to close in on my head but I harshly slapped her thigh making her jolt them open wider as I continuously slurped up her intoxicating juices moaning into her pussy enjoying her taste.

When Harley went back on mute she leaned her head back giving the perfect view of her neck and perfectly sculpted sharp jawline. She began moaning a variety of french words I couldn't understand.

I lifted her blouse up to see her stomach tightly clenching indicating she was about to finally cum.

She brought her gaze back down to me telling me something with her eyes before getting herself together to mutter a few more words to the people in the meeting, she harshly closed the laptop and met my eyes grabbing a fist full of my hair shoving me closer as she let out the girliest moan I've ever heard as she came. She heaved and let go of my hair while I cleaned her up and made my way up to her lips letting her have a taste of herself in a slow kiss.

That didn't last long since I was harshly shoved against her desk moments later.

I watched her fully step out of her trousers, when she was done she brought me onto her lap. Her fingers traced my features as her lips were stuck in between her teeth, her thumb came down on my bottom lip gently tugging at it and letting it go with a bounce. Her lips now hovered over my ear as she was about to say three little words that meant we'd be here longer than expected.

"Ride my thigh."

Two hours later we were all cleaned up and I was forcing Harley to take me to the mall so I could get my parents and cousin who was more of like a niece to me some clothing and souvenirs.

We were hand in hand on the elevator that was taking us down a couple floors too many.

"The hell are we going? This isn't the way to your car" I questionably looked up at her.

"It's the garage my love" And as of on que the elevator doors opened revealing a garage larger than her own apartment, the garage consisted of many sports cars varying from Austin martins to Bugattis.

She led me to a green Mclaren Artura and helped me inside before going to the drivers side after I muttered a 'thank you.'

"You hear the word 'mall' and get the brilliant idea of driving a two seater sports car?" I sighed.

"Not impressed?" Her brow perked up as she started the engine and pressed a button to open the garage.

I looked over at her slightly veiny but feminine hands on the steering wheel "It's just a car. Everything better fit in the trunk or Im banning you banning you from sex and kisses" I reverted my gaze out the window feeling a warm hand on my thigh "It will I promise" she said squeezing the flesh.

I hummed "Both hands on the wheel sweetheart."

She chuckled putting her hand back on the wheel. Within 15 minutes we were at the mall and I sent her off to do what whatever she wanted, I didn't want her trying to pay for everything I don't wanna seem like I'm using her so to ensure I'd be paying for my families gifts I made her leave me be until I said otherwise.

I went into a couple store putting together outfits for my niece then went on to buy my mother a designer item and clothes, my father is a simple man and would be happy with just cologne so I got him that along with a pair of shoes and a watch along with clothes.

The was total of everything was lengthy but nothing I wouldn't earn back.

Dammit I sound like Harley.

I called Harley and when I met her at the water fountain she was carrying two bags and said one was specifically for me, something she picked out and that i had to wait until later to see. She kept her promise of ensuring everything would fit into her trunk.

She drove back to her apartment which I've come to realize is always empty besides us being the only ones to enter and exit the building.

"How come I never see any other tenants leave the building?" I asked as she parked and grabbed the bags leading me into the elevator.

She answered without looking at me "Don't question it, I own it.Being a realtor has its perks."

I didn't say anything and just followed her out.

We began packing our suitcases and cuddling until it hit 6pm.

We took a taxi to the airport and checked in our bags and did the typical airport hassle by then we had a couple minutes until boarding. Paris is never not busy.

Harley held my hand the whole time 'just in case' I got 'lost.'

I knew it was because she'd get jealous if someone tried to talk to me but I'd let her have it I've been traumatized enough by the women here.

We finally boarded and this time I picked economy, I wanted to feel like a regular person again and not spoiled, I'm just surprised she hasn't complained yet but I think I jinxed it.

12

"Why didn't you tell me it was economy? I could've paid for first class or something" She groaned as a baby started wining.

There weren't even that many people on the flight based on the amount of people who were at the gate.

I rolled my eyes "You're so damn spoiled."

"I'm not spoiled I just like nice things" She fanned herself.

"Well, looks I'm stuck on a 16 hour flight with you, again." I intertwined her fingers with mine smiling at the thought of last time.

Chapter 23

Iris POV

"Soooo, wanna join the mile high club?" My girlfriend asked obviously expecting me to agree.

I shoved her face away "After you fucked that gringa in the bathroom last time? No thanks. Ask again and my foot will be up your ass."

She muttered a sorry and briefly kissed my lips before interlocking our fingers.

"Nervous to meet them?" I questioned as she tucked a strand of hair behind my ear "Nope, I can't wait to meet them. I'm sure they're just as great as you." She smiled flashing her perfectly aligned teeth.

Everything about her is perfect from her button nose to her smooth ivory skin, to her pink tinted full lips that were always soft every time they met mine. Even her nails were always clean and manicured with a clear finish. She's my own personal goddess I just so happen to be dating.

I rested my head on her shoulder closing my eyes and engulfing in her warmth as her arms wrapped around me "Nah they aren't but I'll let them have it. Wake me up when we're about to land, I like watching the landing" I yawned immediately dozing off.

"Rory!" I dropped my suitcase and ran to the 15 year old attempting to pick her up.

"Iris! I've missed you so much it's so damn boring here without you" The teens voice muffled into my hair.

Rory let go and moved back curiously eyeing Harley "Who's that sexy lady who keeps looking around as if she's lost?"

"My girlfriend."

She gasped throwing her hand over her mouth in shock.

"Wow."

"Wow?"

"Yeah, I mean she looks really rich like really rich. You sure she isn't your sugar mommy? You don't have to lie ya know, I still kept that secret you told me to keep 10 years ago when I caught you and that girl—

I covered her mouth with my hand daring her to continue.

"Go entertain her while I go find my parents and please don't say anything stupid" I playfully pinched her cheeks walking away in search of my parents.

It didn't take long to find my mom in the kitchen, her happy place.

I quietly snuck behind her covering her eyes with my hands "Guess who" I sung out trying not to laugh at her slightly jumping.

"My favorite child?" The shorter woman joked.

"Your only child but sure I'll take it. Where's papa?" I questioned as she engulfed me in a bone crushing hug.

"Who knows. Probably trying to fix that truck of his for the hundredth time . He'll be in soon, dinner is almost ready go freshen up then we'll talk. We've missed you" She turned back around after kissing my cheek and went back to focus on her favorite task, cooking.

I'm so homesick.

After successfully sneaking Harley pass the kitchen and into the room that was apparently mine according to my mother— we freshened up just in time for dinner.

No one had been at the table yet except for Rory.

"I can't wait to see your moms reaction to this sexy creature you call your girlfriend" Rory sighed placing her arms behind her head.

Harley scratched her head "Uh thanks?"

I rolled my eyes just as my parents entered the dinner room in which they hadn't noticed Harley yet.

I cleared my throat gaining my mothers attention.

She practically threw the salad bowl onto the table when she noticed her.

"Iris!" My mother shrieked.

"Es esta tu mami de azúcar?"

"That's what I said!" Rory pitched in.

"No, mamá, mi novia" I sighed looking over at a very puzzled Harley gently squeezing her hand.

"¿¡Novia!?"

I narrowed my eyes at Rory a snickering Rory shutting her up "Sí, ahora saluda, apuesto a que ya se siente incómoda."

"What's your name?" My dad suddenly butt in cutting off my mother and I.

"Harley."

"See, her name is just as pretty as her face" I grinned grabbing her jaw lightly pecking her lips gaining a fake gag from Rory.

My mother sent Harley a soft smile "Well.. if Iris likes you then I guess you're pretty special. Make yourself comfortable, we're friendly."

My family was sure to stick to their words and made her feel comfortable and welcome alongside Rory's flirty remarks often ignored by us.

"And the night before I asked her to be my girlfriend we were at the pool relaxing and talking then we just started making ou—"

"Here's a pupusa try it" I shoved it in her mouth muffling her before she said any more rancid details of our first time together.

"I never would've thought my Iris would ever give anyone the chance but here we are, you're a lucky one but I must warn you about women and their temper tantrum's" My dad rubbed his temples as if stressed.

Harley scoffed "Tell me about it she's already had like 6."

"Excuse me?"

She looked my way wide eyed and began caressing my thigh "I'm joking she's an angel. Like 70 percent of the time" she whispered the last part to herself.

Asshole.

Chapter 24

Harley's POV

"Please don't make me go down that" I pleaded as Rory was screeching as she went down the massive rainbow slide.

"Don't be such a pussy come on" Iris tugged me towards the cushion eyeing me to sit on it.

I obviously obliged.

She scares me.

Iris sat in front of me in-between my legs with her legs up to her chin.

Our hands both tightly gripped the sides of the cushion and within no time we were sliding down the colorful slide

My heart damn near dropped to my ass when we got to the steepest part but I managed to avoid screaming like a little girl by closing my eyes the whole time.

Iris's hair was flying everywhere including my face.

By time we were at the bottom I was removing a good amount of her hair away from my face.

As we got up and headed towards Rory who was ridiculously dressed in a blow up cow costume I started to look around at all the other different costumes people were wearing today.

"Are we done for the day? You're embarrassing me with that costume of yours" I scoffed at Rory ensuring no one I knew was around even though we were in a entirely different country.

She crossed her arms "No. I still want to go trick-or-treating and the both of you are taking me."

"What do you need a chaperone for? You're 15 why are you still going trick or treating in the first place?"

"Because I have no friends, duh." The teen gave me a look as if it was obvious she had no friends.

I never took her as the type to have to no friends.

"You have to take me. Don't you wanna make a good impression on your girlfriends favorite person" Rory attempted to give me her best puppy eyes.

Iris wrapped a arm around her shuffling us to continue walking "Are you trying to blackmail my girlfriend Rory?"

"Whaaat? Never. Can we go now I swear little kids take all the good candy" And with that Rory grabbed both our hands practically dragging us towards the car.

"I can't believe you're making me do this."

Rory snickered "Go on, knock on the door and say truco o trato."

Why do I feel as if she's trying to set me up? I'm way too old for this and my girlfriend isn't paying us any attention so she can't even save me.

I sighed raising my fist setting my knuckles on the door and lightly knocked.

A short older woman with graying roots appeared with a comforting smile on her face.

I mumbled a quick truco o trato knowing it didn't mix well with my accent.

"Speak up we can't hear you" The teen teased causing me to send her the finger when Iris looked the other way.

Rory gasped clenching her chest.

The woman just stood there saying nothing which means she most likely didn't understand me.

Iris scoffed ushering me it away "My god can we just go we're wasting the poor lady's time" She apologized grabbing a few candies tossing them into Rory's basket.

"You two act like 5 year olds" My girl huffed gripping us by the ears dragging us away from the house.

About hour later we've gotten candies from a few more houses and called it a night since Iris's parents were making dinner.

I'll have to admit trick or treating was funner than I thought even though I teased Rory about it. It was nice spending quality time with Iris and someone I know who's important to her who will soon be just as important to me as is to her. I'm enjoying her family and it's good to know love within a family does actually exist.

"See that wasn't so bad now was it Harley?"

I playfully waved her off "Zip it child."

"Rude. Mom says there's some type of surprise waiting for us" Rory mentioned as she shoved candy into her mouth.

"Please stop talking with your mouth full. I swear it'll take a saint to tame you" Iris said as she peeked through the rearview mirror but Rory ignored her and continued talking about random nonsense but I enjoyed their company.

10 minutes later we reached Iris's parents house hearing laughter all the way from the front door.

When we walked through the door Rory pushed through us, towards the dining table but stopped in her tracks.

"Woah."

Iris made her way towards her "What is it Rory?"

But Iris also stopped in her tracks.

"Holy fucking shit" She mumbled.

What's going on?

I became curious and made my way towards where they were not getting any further then they got.

"Miss me?"

You've got to be fucking kidding me.

Chapter 25

Harley POV

Is she fucking serious!?

She's bringing this shit here.

To Iris's family's home.

Mind you it's my first time meeting them.

Imagine the impression I'm gonna leave on them after this.

Iris leaned into me "Let's just sit and enjoy our food, ignore her" she whispered dragging her fingers down my forearm engulfing my hand with hers leading us to the to the sink to wash our hands then to the table which Rory was already at sorting her halloween candy.

She's such a dork but the more I get to know her the more I want to protect her with my life.

I can't believe she doesn't have any friends?

Everyone was now seated at the table digging into the meal Iris taking a spoonful of some type of rice.

She moaned into the spoon "Here try this babe" she insisted guiding her spoon towards my mouth as I obviously obliged engulfing the spoon into my mouth moaning as well.

I knew what she was doing and I 1000% support.

"Mm it is good, almost as good as you" I whispered the last part to her hoping Sylvia heard.

She— Sylvia cleared her throat and tried to stir up a conversation with my girlfriend.

"So Iris, when do you plan on coming back to Texas?" The annoying woman I used to see as a mother figure asked Iris.

Iris ignored the woman "Mom did you hear something?"

"Mija be nice to your guest, she says she came all the way down here from Cannes to see you."

My brow perked at this information.

Weren't me and Iris just there... Less than 3 days ago.

"Actually mother we're far from friends—"

She tried to defend but was cut off by the woman who's voice sounded almost like mine.

"Indeed far from friends. We were actually seeing each other—"

Iris cut her off slamming her hands on the table.

"The fuck we were you're obsessed with me, admit it. You're a horrible person who humiliates her daughter, harass me and fucking follows me everywhere. You're almost 50 Sylvia god you don't need me and you need to grow the fuck up and understand we don't want you here, you ruin everything fuck you ruined her childhood, you almost ruined her. If you'd just fucking leave us be everything would be fine, why can't you just leave us alone" Iris shouted at the starstruck woman.

She definitely didn't tell a lie though.

I stood placing my palm on her lower back trying to calm her down not knowing if I should step in.

"Iris it's fine I can deal with my mother" I insisted.

Sylvia scoffed "Oh suck it up Iris you know you feel something for me."

"The hell I do" Iris narrowed her eyes.

Sylvia got up from her seat rounding the table and leaned into Iris sizing her up "Do I have to prove it to you? Do I have to remind you how much you wanted me—"

Sylvia's words were cut short by a punch— a punch by none other than I.

"You won't fucking touch her" I spat at the woman now holding her face as she laid on the ground.

I didn't even punch her that hard.

Iris's family sat at the table speechless.

Her fathers eyes wide and confused.

Her mothers face plastered with concern and then there's Rory.

Unphased popping candy into her mouth as she enjoyed the drama as if it was a movie.

I quickly looked away suppressing a chuckle.

Iris's mother sat up from the table rubbing her temples.

"I think it's time for you to go Sylvia, I see I've made a mistake. You're not welcome into my house anymore so go before I take matters into my own hands for you harassing my daughter and daughter-in-law " She pointed towards the door.

Sylvia slowly got up from the hard floor and thanked Iris's mother for the food apologizing to her on her way out.

But before she was fully at the door she turned and looked at me.

You'll pay.

Chapter 26

Harley POV

It's now the next day and I'm currently in the kitchen with Iris's mom helping her prep for lunch.

Rory's currently at school and it'd soon be time for her to get back— less than 30 minutes.

I can say I've enjoyed my time here in El Salvador especially since I've gotten to meet the most important people in Iris's life.

And they just so happen to love me and show me what it's like to actually have people you can call family care about you and I couldn't ask for anything better.

My thoughts were soon cut off by a gentle tap "Mind prepping the table for me?" My mother in law asked.

"Of course."

I grabbed the amount of plates and utensils needed and adroitly placed them around the table.

By time I was placing the finishing touch— the napkins next to the plates the front door was being opened and soon slammed shut revealing a angry Rory who soon made her way back out the back door.

The sudden ruckus caused me to stop in my tracks.

What could possibly make her so angry?

I followed her out of back door just to find her sitting on the last step with her face resting in her hands.

"Rory? Is everything okay?"

Fuck that was a dumb question.

"No. Everything isn't." She mumbled into her palm.

The shorter girl groaned "Wanna talk about it?"

A moment of silence passed without a answer.

It made me feel awkward but I still wanted the teen to know I was there for her whether she wanted to talked about it or not.

"Remember when I said I had no friends?" She sighed.

I had no time to reply before she started again.

"I had a best friend, I'd known her since I could walk. Last year, Freshman year she started acting differently towards me as in flirting being touchy and vulnerable and so fucking cute. She'd be affectionate with me and it made me happy, she knows everything about me, We'd spend nights at her house having fun, talking and cuddled up against each other without a care in the world but then I had realized something no one would even bare having to realize— I had feelings for her and when she kissed me at a party that was just the cherry on top. It'd taken me months to even build the courage to bring it up to her and when I finally did shit went downhill— she said her kisses meant nothing, our hugs meant nothing, my vulnerability meant nothing and I'd never mean anything more to her. It was just fun for her; harmless. After the interaction I just left and the next day at school she ignored me, I didn't exist to her. It was the start of my bullying, the start of everyone treating me differently—looking at me differently. I wasn't human to them anymore. They say hurtful shit Harley I don't think you understand how fucking mean people are, they push me around, knock food out of my hands and get me in trouble with the teachers. I could bare it because I won't even know them in a couple years but today I'd just had enough."

I engulfed the sniffling girl into my arms— comforting her not interrupting her once.

She then went on to say.

I'm being bullied because I like girls.

Chapter 27

Harley POV

I still held Rory in my arms as she began calming down.

It's now been a good 10 minutes since she told me how she'd been getting treated at school and to say I felt for her was a understatement.

Why do people worry so much about people who like the same gender? It shouldn't phase them.

It was clear she didn't want me to say anything and that she just needed to be comforted which is what I didn't hesitate to do. Plus I'm pretty sure no one else knew about the situation since she said she'd been tolerating it.

I wouldn't want my kid being treated like this, hell I'd go crazy trying to protect them.

But I could see why she hadn't said anything to anyone yet— either she didn't want anyone to make a big deal out of it or she just wasn't out yet.

Around the time Rory sat up and wiped her eyes Iris's silhouette filled the space of the door as she called out to us.

"Dinner's ready— is everything okay?" She asked paused mid sentence.

I gave her a look which could only mean not to question it.

She got the idea and left us be soon after giving me a questionable look.

I stood up from the uncomfortable step dusting off my now aching ass.

"Don't worry Rory, I'm apart of your family now and I care about you. I'll handle it okay?"

She nodded heading up the stairs soon after not even questioning it.

I really hope what i'm about to do helps her recover.

"What was that all about? Earlier i mean" Iris questioned as she began removing her jeans.

"I really don't think i should be saying anything since she came to me about but i can ensure i'll be handling it tomorrow therefore i'll be out quite awhile" She nodded as I walked towards her engulfing her hair and tugged connecting our lips soon after.

She stepped out of her pants and i immediately slid my hands into her underwear running two fingers over her slit causing her to bite down on my bottom lip.

"Go wait in the shower for me?"

She groaned "Harls, we can't, not in my mom's house."

"Shh i know it's just a innocent shower, i'm saving you for when we get back to Paris" I removed my now wet fingers.

She hummed pecking my lips heading to the shower not long after my eyes lingering after her.

I threw myself on the bed sighing.

The emotions i feel for her are so unreal.

It hasn't even been three months and i feel like this.

Am i falling in love with iris?

Chapter 28

Harley POV

After hours of paperwork and conversations with higher ups i finally wrote my signature on the last line sighing and dropping the pen.

The greying man nodded his head looking towards my translator who just made me aware of the basics once again and that copies of the paperwork would be sent to iris's parents before we left back to France.

I looked to my translator "C'est un plaisir de travailler avec vous, j'espère être un atout pour la communauté scolaire." I smiled to the man gathering my things and headed out the office soon after.

The Salvadoran air right now was warm and congested but the sun was out which brightened my mood especially since that meeting went swiftly.

Now all i had to do was get to Rory's school.

I made my way into the black truck and instructed him to drive me to the teens school.

We arrived within half an hour and i then instructed him to wait outside instead of having to drive all the way back.

I got out the truck and made my way into the school and into the office eyeing everyone to which i also saw a few people packing their things and leaving meaning they were aware of the news.

i really should've thought this through especially since i didn't have the translator anymore.

I pulled out my phone and pulled up google translate typing "Everyone get the fuck out you're all fired if you hadn't noticed already."

Some ushered out in a hurry and other just gasped in disbelief.

I then typed into google translate again "If you're still here i'm assuming you're confused. Get the hell out!!!" I added the exclamation points so they'd know to take me serious.

When the office was finally cleared I made to way to the intercom hovering my phone speaker over it "If you're the little the shit who outed my girls niece i expect you in the office in the next 10 seconds or you'll regret every life choice you've ever made and yes, maybe this is a threat but for legal reasons it isn't now hurry up you have 4 seconds."

And with that i relaxed in the chair sighing as i waited for the girl.

I eventually heard footsteps but when i looked up it wasn't the girl, it was Rory who had a puzzled expression written over her face.

"My god Harley what are you doing here?" She asked.

I smiled "Well i did say i'd handle it didn't i."

"You did but you know iris is going to freak out right" She chuckled sitting across from me.

Another pair of footsteps approached us and a puzzled girl entered the room.

Her and Rory made eye contact Rory looking away immediately after.

I took it as we should probably go.

"You can leave, i'll torture you another day." I waved her off.

She just eyed me up and down rolling her eyes as she walked out.

That little shit.

I got up from my new seat at my new desk in my new office smiling at my impulsive decision.

Rory soon followed dusting off her pants "So you bought the school Harley?"

I hummed making my way towards the exit as she followed me out.

"I did, now what do you say we go get ice cream?"

We're currently walking back to the truck from ice cream parlor.

I watched as the teen tripped over absolutely nothing;air but still somehow managed to drop a scoop of her ice cream on the ground.

I covered my mouth and looked the opposite direction in attempt to stop myself from laughing.

I opened the truck door signaling her to get in "Please don't spill any of that in the truck or you'll be cleaning it" I glared at her even though she ignored me.

I sighed and made my way to the other side of the truck preparing myself for my unpredictable girlfriend.

"Scared?" The teen smirked.

"Of her? Tuh never she's like 5ft" I scoffed looking back out the window.

"She's not going to hurt me right?"

Rory just smiled turning her gaze back out the window.

Officially scared.

-

Chapter 29

Rory POV

I watched Iris chased an out of breathe Harley around the kitchen as i sat on the couch spectating.

"Ven aquí, no te haré daño por ser tan jodidamente descuidada." Iris shouted from across the room holding a house shoe.

You see, i warned the french woman ahead of time to which she ensured she wasn't afraid of Iris but their cat and mouse game proved otherwise.

I eventually got bored of them and made my way back to my room.

I threw myself onto my bed face first hoping the mattress would just engulf me forever.

Being a teenager is so fucking hard.

When we made eye contact everything came rushing back.

The feelings, sadness, defeat but the anger and hatred overpowered and i knew i'd never forgive her nor did i want to.

I need to move on.

Shit i'm still in disbelief Harley went out of her way to buy my school.

If she could do that for me i could just imagine how much she'd do for Iris.

I could tell they loved each other even if they'd not told each other yet, it was obvious.

i've never seen Iris give anyone including women the time of day nor have i ever seen her so visibly happy.

So seeing how they interact with one another makes me feel for them even if i do occasionally yearn.

I just don't think i could get close to anyone like that again. I owe it to myself.

I need to promise myself to protect myself and put myself before others so they can never get the chance to hurt me or embarrass me again.

I sat up reaching for my remote turning on euphoria then began doing some school work.

20 minutes into my work i got a knock on my door and in came Iris.

Let's just say she came in at typical Nate and Maddy interaction.

"What the fuck are you watching?" She sat at the end of my bed obviously judging my choice of entertainment.

"A masterpiece. Something you obviously wouldn't understand therefore i won't bother explaining myself" I shrugged pausing the show.

She scoffed "Right... Anyways do you maybe want to tell me why my girlfriend bought your school which is about 1 Million dollars by the way?"

"Well since it was a question, no." I dragged the L throwing myself back on the bed only to receive a very aggressively thrown stuffed animal thrown at my head.

"Hey! Don't throw her that's Winnie" I swung my pillow at her only for her to yank it away from my grip.

I groaned giving up trying to beat up the 24 year old.

I brought Winnie up to my chest positioning her under my chin securing my grip on her finally answering her question.

"She bought it because of Elise."

"Oh my god. The fucker with the thinning hair? What did she do?"

"Sheesh insults already? I hadn't even told you what happened yet."

"No need. She's automatically wrong now what did she do?"

I rolled my eyes continuing "She outed me after leading me on for months which resulted in the entire school bullying me and throwing shit on me whenever they felt necessary. She still somewhat means something to me so i can't find it in me to do anything about it or.. hurt her no matter how much she's been hurting me" I whispered the last part to myself not wanting to vocalize how much of a pussy i am when it comes to her even if she doesn't even hesitate to hurt me.

Does this mean i felt some sort of non-platonic love for her?

If so, i don't ever want to experience these feelings ever again.

Iris ushered me towards her adjusting my head to rest on her shoulder as she ran her manicured hands through my hair.

"Why didn't you tell me?" She genuinely asked.

She can't be serious though?

"Iris i hate to break it to you but you're fucking crazy."

"Am not! I'm perfectly normal."

I chuckled at her attempt to convince me she doesn't have insane tendencies "I don't know who you're fooling but it isn't me."

"Whatever, No wonder Harls did what she did but seriously Rory you shouldn't have to think twice about defending yourself no matter if you love that person or not. If they loved you or cared about you as much as you did then they wouldn't make you feel even an ounce of helpless, sad or hurt. It's okay to care and not want to hurt the one you love but when it comes to things like this, when it comes to someone being selfish and stupid you don't hesitate to fucking defend yourself okay?"

I just hummed not wanting to talk about it anymore.

She rested her head on top of mine "Please tell me next time? So i can strangle that fucker."

"See? This is exactly what i was talking about not normal." I replied as i attempted to win the fight against me heavy eyes.

"I'm gonna sleep now, you should go apologize to your girlfriend for chasing her around the house with a house shoe like the manic you at."

She hopped up sending me the finger "Fuck you. You're right though sweet dreams kid i love you."

"Love you more. And Iris? What'd you say if i stayed with you back in the states for awhile.. Just to get away for a couple months? Abuela and Abuelo are getting too old to care for me nowadays."

Iris let out a slightly inaudible screech of excitement.

"I thought you'd never ask."

We let that be and as soon as she closed the door i pressed play on euphoria.

I fucking love Lexi.

Chapter 30

Iris POV

My girlfriend currently had her hands cupped over my mothers smaller hands saying her final goodbye and who knows what else.

I brought the almost taller teen to me engulfing her tightly.

"Just 2 more weeks and you'll be spending the summer with us, okay?" My words muffled from my face being shoved into her hair.

She hummed pulling away almost looking sad.

"I love you Rory, this'll be the best summer ever. I promise" I stuck my pinky finger out wrapping it around hers.

After ruffling her hair I kissed my parents on the cheek grabbing Harley's hand shortly after.

After situating ourselves in the car i laid my head on her shoulder going over my plan to surprise her.

We may be gay but i wasn't about to be in a relationship that formed over sex especially with a woman i finally had enough interest in to pursue.

So i was going to do it right. Soon.

But only after i found out how we were going to be in a long distance relationship.

i'd just bring it up when we get back to her apartment.

As soon as we walked through the doors of her placid apartment my lips were being attacked by even softer ones followed with a body that led us towards the bedroom

As soon my back hit the soft white sheets my girlfriend began sucking on my jaw her leg between my own apply pressure where i wanted her for the past week.

"Harley" I attempted to say through a moan.

My girl questionably hummed continuing her work which i'm sure was to make a hickey.

I pushed her off as gentle as i could to which her face plastered concern immediately.

"Baby wait" I huffed trying to catch my breath.

She immediately began caressing my forearm.

"What's wrong amore? Talk to me."

Goodness the point was to have a conversation about the distance we would soon have but i can't help but feel enamored with how gentle she's beings right now.

I pushed myself back towards the headboard patting the spot next to me.

"I just wanted to get something that's been bothering me off my chest."

Her right eyebrow perked up indicating she wasn't going to interrupt and for me to continue.

I sighed folding my legs.

"Wait you aren't breaking up with me right?" The French woman worriedly joked.

I chuckled grabbing her chin and bringing her lips to mine.

She pulled back soon after, still concerned.

She narrowed her eyes "Iris"

"No baby, i'm not. Just listen okay?"

She immediately relaxed beginning to fiddle with my finger waiting for me to start talking again.

"You're aware i only came here for a short vacation right?" She nodded repeatedly separating my fingers.

I continued "And I live back in Texas, which is in America."

Harleys smart comment cutting me off "Wow thanks for the clarification" she playfully scoffed.

I rolled my eyes continuing "And you live back here, In France."

"Are you just going to keep saying things i already know?"

This woman.

"Well if you'd stop cutting me off i could get through what i need to say" I narrowed my eyes at the difficult woman.

"Fine. I'll shut up"

"Thank you. As i was trying to say we live in two different countries all the way on the opposite sides of the world and i really need to get back soon, for work. And i just don't know how it'll work. Of course i thought about it before we even got fully entangled with one another but i pushed it to the back of my mind because i didn't want the time i spent with you to end. Realistically it did have to be brought up so i'm doing it now. I don't know how well we'll do so far from each other but i—"

My sentence being cut off again by almost strident "No"

"You can live here Iris. You don't have to go back or work anymore. Just be with me, let me—"

"Harley i'm not allowing myself to be disabled by you. I have to do something, i want to work i can't just sit at home all day wherever "home" is and let you do everything i have a family which you just met i have to provided for and i sure as hell am not going to be some housewife so if that's all you can resort to then i don't know what to tell you."

Harley let go of my hand she was fiddling with seconds before.

"So that's it? You don't agree with one thing i say and now you don't know? You don't know what? If you can be with me anymore?" The taller woman stood not even waiting for my response before grabbing a towel and exiting the room.

Who the hell does she think she is to just walk away from me?

As soon i heard the shower in the other room running i got up and made my way there.

Her clothes scattered all over the floor of the steamy bathroom.

Goodness the mirror was already sweating.

Is she literally trying to give herself 1st degree burns.

I pulled the curtains to the side revealing a naked Harley with her head resting on the wall letting the scorching water run over her curly hair down her body.

"Don't walk away from me you asshole. Talk" I demanded trying my best to ignore the way her abs clenched under the hot water.

She ignored me keeping her eyes shut.

I reached in front of her turning off the water which immediately got her to acknowledge my presence.

"You look like a stupid try hard with your head on the wall like that and if you aren't going to talk to me no water for you." I huffed crossing my arms.

She reached for the knob turning the water on again and soon harshly closed the curtains in my face.

Is she serious right now..

I sighed in annoyance at her childishness but if she wants to be that way then fine.

My hand reached for the curtain pulling it back and reaching for the knob turning the water off again.

My stubborn girl then turned it back on shutting the curtain again.

I saw the way her jaw ticked each time we went back in forth with the curtain.

I honestly found it amusing how we'd been going back in forth for the past few minutes.

I eventually gave up mumbling a "fine" under my breath.

I was going to get her to talk to me one way or another.

I removed my jeans, sweater and undergarments moving the gray curtain to the side once more gaining the french woman's attention as i joined her under the scorching water.

"Iris i swear to god—" She spoke through her teeth but her sentence was cut short as she took in my naked body.

Chapter 31

Harley POV

I groaned turning away from the alluring womans body closing my eyes as i retook my position under the hot water which was likely on the verge of creating blisters on my skin.

My shorter girl mumbled something about me acting like a child under her breath but i just ignored it shutting the hot water off and making my way out.

If i stayed any longer or looked at her bare body just waiting for me i would've gave into fucking her.

Which was not apart of my evening plans.

I reached for my towel on the shelf just for it to be snatched seconds before i could grab it.

Iris stuck her tongue out at me as she wrapped the towel around herself walking out soon after.

I only sighed and made my way to my room butt naked water droplets trialing from the bathroom to my bedroom floor.

We got dressed in silence and whilst doing so guilt washed over me.

Maybe i should hear her out.

Maybe i was just jumping to conclusions and she had a better solution for us— as a couple.

Deciding to let my thoughts take over in the kitchen instead of letting them roam i decided to make us a quick lunch.

I made my way to my kitchen taking a shot before getting started on our lunch which would consist of a salad and fruit assorted crepes.

After a good 15 minutes i went to fetch my girl.

I walked into the room to see her standing in front of a mirror brushing her dark waist length hair.

Flashbacks of our time on the boat resurfaced causing heat to arise in my body.

I cleared my throat gaining the attention of the latin girl.

"I made lunch. Come." I practically demanded leaving the room shortly after annoyed at the little attitude i still couldn't seem to get rid of.

I sat at my island waiting for the shorter woman who appeared from around the corner seconds later.

She sat and we silently began eating.

"I should fucking strangle you for your nonsense behavior" she scoffed.

I perked my right brow intrigued as to how she could possibly 'strangle' me "Oh? How so Iris?"

"Don't test me." She nonchalantly stuffed her face full of salad after.

I stood to my full height leaning over the island.

Iris stood too— our faces now inches apart.

"Go ahead, do it. Strangle me, I dare" My breathe surely fanning her face.

She smirked lifting her palm surely about to wrap it around my neck but i instead caught her hand with my left and gripped a fist full of her hair with my right pulling her even closer to me.

My girl let out an unexpected gasp at my swift aggressiveness.

I was caught off guard when her other hand still managed to wrap around my neck.

"Touché" I rolled my eyes at her still managing to 'strangle' me.

Iris hummed looking as if she was fighting with herself in her head.

"I'm still mad at you but you just look too fucking good right now" Her lips devoured mine as soon as she finished her sentence.

Within seconds she climbed over the island sitting on her knees while my hand still gripped her hair and her soft palms held my face in place.

I trailed a line of kisses down her jaw to her neck to her shoulder blades.

"I seen a little something in your closet. Go get it. Then after you fuck me with it it'll be you i'll have moaning, okay?" My girl got through her soft moans.

I wasted no time and made my way to my room and back in records time.

I sat the black rectangular box with sleek silver calligraphy writing down next to my eager woman.

I opened the box to reveal a 8 inch strap quite close to my skin tone.

She took no time in 'helping' me remove my joggers though she damn near yanked them off lifting her oversized shirt seconds after.

Iris grazed her tongue over her bottom lip "Come on baby, what's the hold up?"

Fuck me.

Chapter 33

Harley POV

I hooked my arms around her thicker thighs pulling her towards the edge of the kitchen island.

Deciding on a little foreplay i leaned forward capturing her full pink lips in an intense kiss.

Her tongue overtaking mine for a split second before i let go of one of her thighs only to wrap the unoccupied hand around her neck.

"Don't."

Her eyes challenging mine deciding whether or not to go against my words.

She only nodded wrapping her smaller hand around mine around her neck.

"If you're going to choke me do it harder" She smirked.

I rolled my eyes at her but listened.

She led my hand from her bare chest down to her pussy—spreading her wetness with my fingers intentionally grazing her clit.

My girl threw her head back softly moaning at the sensation.

I only admired the pretty sounds she made.

Her long dark lashes covering her brown doe eyes.

Her full pink bottom lip being attacked by her teeth.

Her chest heaving up and down— her breast bouncing a little— the pattern of her chest intriguing me.

Deciding she's had enough of teasing herself i sharply readjusted her wrist to the sides of her hips.

"Ready mon amour?" My woman eagerly nodded.

Focused— i regained my position around her thighs concentrated on perfectly aligning the toy with her opening.

I wanted my girl to be as comfortable as she could be.

Even if she unfortunately may be experienced before me i still wanted to give her the best experience possible.

I slowly entered her her mouth agape immediately.

I covered her lips with mine feeling the vibration of her moans against my lips as i eased the strap inside her inch by inch.

I slowly moved my hips getting her used to the stretch.

Then i went ballistic in no time.

I'd make it up to her later but right now i needed to put her in her place.

I hiked her leg high on my waist gaining me better access.

I thrusted the strap deeper— her clit reaching the base surely adding to the sensations she felt.

My girl letting out a scream as i fucked her.

She whispered an 'I'm close' so i flipped her on her stomach pushing down on her back getting her to arch for me.

The view of her pussy from here made my mouth water.

I'm definitely tasting her after this.

Iris clawed at the marble counter eagerly pushing her hips back causing the strap the occasionally graze my clit eliciting a barely audible groan from me.

I grabbed a fist full of her hair pulling and thrusting harder.

She came undone in seconds screaming at the top of her lungs.

"Why are you so fucking good at that" Iris groaned —trying to catch her breath as she turned over on her back.

I shushed her "Oh we aren't done yet my love, spread your legs for me and watch me eat you."

Iris did just that as i ate her again and again making her cum 3 other times.

And yes, she indeed did have me on this counter moaning for her.

We laid in bed cuddled up and holding each other after our short 4 hour session in my kitchen.

I gently kissed the side of her head as she peacefully slept.

I only watched her.

I find the most beautiful state of someone— especially Iris to be when she's asleep.

Unaware of how beautiful she looks.

When she wakes up i know we'll have to revisit the moving situation.

I sighed leaning over to grab my phone.

It was hitting 9pm and i definitely worked off our lunch so instead of cooking i'd go out and buy us dinner.

I got up and quickly showered washing the scent of our previous hours off.

I wet my hair and pushed it back deciding i'd let the curls air dry.

I rode the elevator down to my garage and decided to take my BMW out for the night.

When i got to the restaurant i order us almost everything off the menu and headed back as fast as i could.

When i got back into the apartment iris had just gotten out the shower herself and was putting her hair up.

I watched her gracefully stare at herself through the mirror taking notice of me soon after.

"Oh you're back, where'd you go?" She made her way to me wrapping her arms around my neck leaning up to kiss me.

I met her halfway pecking her lips over and over until she pushed me away.

"To get us dinner. I'm sure you've worked off lunch as much as i have" My girl hummed walking past me making her way to the kitchen unboxing all the shit i bought for us.

I sat in one the stools looking over at the island i just fucked her on.

Oh i'll never look at this island the same again.

Chapter 34

Iris POV

I gathered our dishes and placed them in the sink turning on the water letting the dishes soak while i helped Harley clear the island.

When that was finished i began washing the dishes and getting my thoughts together to ensure i knew what i wanted to say without regretting it.

I sighed turning off the faucet when i completed the dishes.

I made my way over to Harley who was sitting on the couch watching American Horror Story.

I sat on her lap wrapping my arms around her stomach with my head resting on her chest.

"You watch the freakiest shit" I mumbled into her perfectly sized chest.

She gasped.

"Just because you judge Rory for watching euphoria doesn't mean you get to judge me for watching this masterpiece" She rolled her eyes mesmerized at the scene of some weird person in a leather suit.

I only hummed thinking about the teenage girl who'd be living with me in no time.

Groaning i spoke "Fuck, speaking of Rory i need to start looking for a bigger apartment."

Harley shifted under me pausing the weird show.

"Well if you'd stay here she could—"

"No."

"Why won't you just hear me out?" The woman mumbled.

"Because you're not thinking logically, you're only thinking about being closer and supporting everything but not what i'd be leaving behind, Harley."

Knowing i was right, she remained silent.

"I can't stay anymore longer than a week, I have to prepare for Rory and getting back into my work space."

"Okay, i know there's no changing your mind. My woman is stubborn but could we at-least do a couple of more things together before you go?" She sighed.

I rolled my eyes at how devastated she sounded.

"We're not breaking up dumbo, just... a little long distance. We're make it work i promise. And of course we can do more things together before i go, i've actually had this one thing planned for awhile" I bit my lip as i stretched one of her curls twirling it around my finger and watching it bounce perfectly back in its place.

"Fuck" Harley let out a sigh of relief.

"I thought we were like— done. Forever" She added.

"Never. You've made my stay here too memorable and fun for me to just live my life and forget about you. Plus how could i ever forget about your precious face" I pinched her cheeks though her face was quite slender and toned.

I fucking love androgynous humans.

She playfully swatted my hand away "Fuck off. Expect me to fly to you every week, not like i have anything else to do."

"Ahh yes rich people problems" I rolled my eyes.

"Speaking of forgetting— i wouldn't dare forget about these magical fingers of yours and that mouth.." I teased caressing her fingers and bringing her lips to mine.

Harley deepened the kiss by threading her fingers in my hair damn near shoving me closer.

She rested her forehead on mine.

Her gaze alone makes me melt.

How could i stay put together when a woman like her looked at me like this?

"I could refresh your memory the rest of the week— if you'd like" She tilted her head with a smirk.

Removing myself from her lap, i pulled her up and led her to the bed.

Pushing her onto it i climbed on top of her— lifting her shirt which revealed her feminine abs.

I began lightly kissing her jaw.

Then made my way toward her ear.

I then confessed "Con el paso de las semanas he llegado a quererte .. mucho pero, no necesitas saberlo. Hasta que llegue el momento mi amor."

Harley looked in awe at me as i lifted my head to look at her.

"I have no idea what you just fucking said to me but.. you're my love too."

I kissed her until she couldn't breathe.

Though that wasn't fully a confession.. It was enough for me until the time was right.

I'm her love and she's mine.

Chapter 35

Harley POV

Kiss.

"I'm going to miss you so much"

Kiss.

"I wish i could just keep you hostage in my apartment"

Kiss.

"Ugh get off" Iris playfully shoved me away

"Jesus I'll still be here another two days"

"Two days is basically two hours" I whined pulling her back to me.

"Are you trying to say you won't miss me as soon as you step on that plane?" I teased grazing my thumb over her bottom lip.

Iris's lashes fluttered down to my touch on her lips— bringing her focus back to me.

She cleared her throat resting her hand over mine guiding it around her waist "Help me pack before we fuck each other and end up late to Disneyland" She pecked my lips and regained her spot on the floor in front of her suitcase.

"Are you saying If i don't help we'll make love?"I sung dragging out the O.

Iris sighed shoving something at me to fold "Almost 30 and act like a teenager" She chuckled.

I gasped "I'm not that old! I have a good 3 years left thank you very much."

"Hey i never said i was complaining" She shrugged.

"Your stamina makes up for it big time" She patted my cheek.

Within an hour we finished packing the things Iris wouldn't be needing the next two days.

We played with Esme for awhile then headed down to my garage and that's when a idea popped inside my head.

"Why are you cheesing like that weirdo?"

I wrapped my arm around her waist bringing her closer to me as we walked to my range rover.

I decided on a larger car since i for sure plan on buying her the largest mickey mouse stuffed animal i can.

"You'll find out when we get back mon amour" I bent down pecking her on the lips.

Iris hummed and made her way into the truck after i opened the door for her.

"Such a gentlewoman" She smirked whilst grabbing her seatbelt.

I gently gripped her chin—bringing her attention to me and grinning down at her "Only for you bébé."

Iris bit her lip and looked away, attempting to hide her blush.

"Better be" My girl mumbled.

Chuckling i made my way to the drivers side— my hand resting on her thigh the entire way there.

"I can't believe you just made me ride in teacups" Iris groaned whilst she wrapped her arm around mine.

"I can't believe you made me put on mickey ears" I retorted.

Iris rolled her eyes and pulled me toward some huge ass rollercoaster.

I couldn't wait to hear her screams and tease her about it.

Within minutes we were next in line and were making our way to our seats.

"Let's see which makes you scream louder, me or the rollercoaster."

"Shut it. I don't scream on rollercoaster—

Iris was cut off by the rollercoaster starting and yanking us forward.

She let out a high pitched scream— covering her mouth as soon as she realized she was proven wrong.

"I don't scream on rollercoasters" I mocked her.

"Fuck you" Iris scoffed—squeezing her eyes shut as we went down a 20ft drop.

Its so fucking weird how little rollercoasters phase me.

Possibly because of the shit i've witnessed my dad get in.

After we got off me and Iris played a couple games and i bought her almost everything in the store.

By time we finished shopping it was getting dark and the light show would be starting

"Hey i'm going to the bathroom, stay here okay?" Iris leaned up pecking my lips— not allowing me to even respond before disappearing.

I sighed but stayed in place as my girl commanded.

Minutes went by but she had yet to return.

In attempt not to freak out i reminded myself I was dating Iris. She could definitely take care of herself.

But what if something happened? What if someone my dad—

My thoughts were cut off by the screen on the castle beaming white.

Mickey coming on soon after.

He had an 'announcement'.

"— And now everybody we have a special guest with a message to her girlfriend" Mickeys annoying voice stated.

Someone rented the screen just to get a message out to their girl? Bold.

Impressed, i gave my full attention to the screen.

Where the fuck is Iris? It's been almost 10 minutes.

I swear god if she's not back at the end of this i'm going to—

"Harley" Iris's voice came from the screen.

How the hell?

"I know you're probably freaking out about where i am right now but i'm here. In front of a bunch of people i don't know but i don't care if hundreds of people see and hear what I'm doing. At least they'll know you're mine, right? To get to the point.. I'm up here to ask you to be my girlfriend the proper way. To confess only the part of my feelings i can get into words for you."

Oh My God.

"Harley Améra Monet, Though i'd never admit it before, i'd been attracted to you since the very moment i saw you, and you knew it. You still managed to get me to fall for you— in these short amount of weeks but i can't say i regret it because, these have been the best few weeks of my life and we've still managed to go through hell together all whilst getting to know each other. To keep it short and simple so these people can get back to their day... Harley.. Will you be my girlfriend? Be mine. Officially?"

Yes.

I shouted "Yes."

I probably looked like a crazy person but i don't give a shit. I'm now, officially dating the woman of my dreams.

Fuck i'm so lucky.

"Assuming you said yes, im going to come find you now and kiss the shit out of you"

And with that everyone clapped and went on to give their attention back to Mickey who appeared on the screen

"Boo"

Iris attempted to jump-scare me

When i turned around she immediately wrapped her arms around my neck— leaning up for that kiss she mentioned earlier.

"Je suis si heureux d'avoir une femme aussi parfaite et belle que toi comme amie. Tu valais bien tout ce que cela impliquait. Iris, je t'ai..."

I began to whisper the last words to myself but resisted.

"Have i ever told you you turn me on when you speak french?" My girlfriend smirked.

"Oh?" I hummed

"About that thing i was thinking about earlier.. want to find out now?" I pushed her hair behind her ear— using my thumb the caress her faint red cheek from the cold.

Iris's eyes held this almost rebellious and mischievous glint in them.

She then went on to answer me after pulling me down to her for another kiss.

Fuck Yes.

Chapter 36

Iris POV

Harley was speeding back to her apartment.

Cutting cars off and cutting lanes all while i was nibbling on her neck leaving little marks.

Harley's jaw ticked "Keep doing that and we're going to crash."

I hummed dragging my finger up and down her trouser covered thigh.

"At least we'll possibly die girlfriends" I slipped my hand under her shirt running my fingers over her abs.

Before Harley could respond she pulled into her garage.

"Get out and sit on the hood with your legs spread, i'll be back." She casually spoke disappearing inside the elevator soon after.

With my shaky legs and throbbing core i made my way to the front of the car and I sat on the hood, as she said.

But instead, i had my legs crossed— tapping the hood of the car with my nails awaiting her return.

Minutes later the elevator dinged signaling her return to which she had a box in her hand.

"Did i have you waiting long princesse?" She sat the box down on top of the car.

My heart almost skipped a beat at the nickname.

Sure she's called me other things but princess is another thing.

I cleared my throat— ready to respond but instead Harley answered herself.

"I don't think so. Why are your legs crossed? That's not what i told you to do now is it?" Her brow perked in curiosity.

"Now what fun would that be? Por qué no las difundes para mí?"

She sighed, hooking her hands under my thighs.

Sharply separating them. She fit herself between my legs— fingers threaded in my hair— eyes locked directly with mine.

"I just did didn't i?" She spoke pulling me closer by the hair.

"You understood me?" My mouth slightly agape in shock.

"I have this whole time chica tonta" She smirked—mocking me.

"Te odio jodidamente" I playfully pushed her away though she barely budged at my shoving attempt.

Chuckling — She repositioned herself— securely wrapping my legs around her waist Harley began leaving little kisses below my jaw.

"Oh but you don't, you love me Iris." She softly whispered repositioning her face in front of mine— holding eye contact once more.

This time, my heart actually felt like it was going to stop.

I harshly swallowed looking away.

How could i hold eye contact with her after she understood me all this time?

She probably heard my failed confession in her sleep.

She is a pretty light sleeper.

"As a business woman Iris, how could i not know multiple languages? Especially Spanish?" She chuckled once more repositioning my head to face her again.

"What is this i'm seeing? Iris nervous? Embarrassed? Impaire"

Sighing, she backed away and took me in.

She leaned forward, resting her forehead on mine tightly shutting her eyes and began speaking.

"Yo también te quiero, ¿sabes? Allí, en el parque, iba a decírtelo pero no quería asustarte ni parecer que iba demasiado rápido."

"I didn't want you to leave with any pressure you know?" She then reopened her eyes.

"Harley. How could i not love after all this time? After everything we've encountered in the short amount of time and still stuck together? Shit how could anyone not.. look at you" I took her in— groaning at the sight.

She's perfect

"Speak for yourself but seriously Iris, I really really adore you" She tucked a hair behind my ear and positioned her mouth in front of mine

"Entonces fóllame como tú" I closed the gap between us and kissed her like i never had before

She let me take control of the kiss for once.

Our tongues coaxing each other. Harley broke the kiss after some time, she swiftly removed my pants and panties all in one motion— repositioning herself in front of my core

"Como quieras" Her raspy voice seductively uttered

"Be as loud as you want. Je veux que tes sons soient gravés dans mon esprit pour ne jamais les oublier pendant ton absence"

As if i needed her permission to be loud.

Harley spread my wetness with her thumb.

Her velvety tongue stuck out— ready to have its first taste all while she held eye contact with me

She didn't fail to keep eyes focused on mine even as i threw my head back in pleasure.

She seemed to want to savor the moment and take her time with me based on her slow she ran her tongue over my clit

Her tongue moved in slow circles

It almost felt like she was spelling her name with her tongue.

Either way my hips began slowly following the rhythm of her tongue.

My moans soft as i focused on her pleasuring me once more.

My girl then brought two of fingers up to my mouth.

"Suck."

I did as told and took them into my mouth— lubing her fingers with my saliva

She gently inserted them inside me pumping slowly

Even this left me a whimpering mess

"I'll only be so gentle after awhile, enjoy it while you can" She suddenly spoke tending back to my clit soon after

"Puedo manejarlo" I managed to get out through my moans.

Harley only chuckled, suctioning her mouth around my clit.

The pressure and pumping combo only made me louder and closer than ever

I unintentionally clawed at the hood of her car whilst tightly shutting my eyes.

My girls fingers sped up as she felt my walls begin to tighten

When i was seconds away from finishing she switched out her fingers for tongue and began fucking me with her tongue

Her tongue thrashed inside me in eagerness

In no time i was finishing inside her mouth.

She cleaned me up— licking her lips and managing eye contact with me while doing so.

"You taste perfect mon amour"

I only hummed bringing her in for a sweet kiss she didn't allow to last for long

"We're not finished so don't get comfortable, okay?" Harley practically stated as she began removing her belt

She took both my wrist in her hands caressing them before the belt made contact with my wrist

She then wrapped the belt around my wrist binding them both together behind my back "Tell me if it's too tight, okay?"

I nodded curious as to what was next to come.

Harley reached for the box removing the top of it to later reveal a new, 8 inch, blue strap.

I watched as she unbuttoned her pants and stepped out of them soon removing her underwear after. She unbuttoned her blouse revealing the sides of her bare chest and exposing her soft feminine abs.

She then adjusted the strap around her waist.

Fuck this is going to be a long night.

Chapter 37

Iris POV

Harley lined up the tip of the strap with my entrance using her unoccupied hand to pin my left leg open.

Her gaze met mine and without warning she pushed herself inside me eliciting a gasp out of me.

"Fuck" I managed to get out through my continuous moans.

Within seconds she began relentlessly thrusting inside me causing me to throw my head back in pleasure.

From our skin slapping together to Harley's grunts our sounds echoed through the garage.

I felt myself getting close and almost as if she could tell too— she stopped.

Harley pulled out of me leaving me shocked and sensitive

She cupped my chin forcing me to look at her "I told you, i wasn't going to be nice very long. Now stand up and turn around me for me"

I closed the gap between us— pouring out all my neediness into the kiss but Harley didn't let that last long

She looked at me, awaiting my response.

"If i don't?" I challenged

Harley's eyes showed a sense of shock but she hid it well.

"Ne soyez pas stupide Iris, you will." And she stepped away— waiting for me to move

I groaned at my defeat and the thought of how wobbly my legs probably are

I slowly slid down the hood of the truck and turned around as she said all while attempting not to fall from my sensitivity

Harley now stood behind me, peppering kissed from my shoulder blade up to my ear

"Buena chica" She softly whispered

My knees buckled at the name and Harley had to support my body weight with her own by pinning my front against the bumper

Chuckling once more she wrapped her hand around my neck—lifting it and gently trailing kisses down my jaw

Without warning again she re-entered meand began thrusting.

Her strokes slow, meaningful and hard.

My moans became louder and i felt closer than ever.

I wasn't sure or Harley was going to edge me again but i took my chance

"Harley." I choked out

She seductively groaned in my ear— she squeezed at my neck tighter causing my moans to become whiny

"Not yet."

"Please." I pleaded

"No." She refused pulling out

I clawed at the hood of the truck from the sudden emptiness i felt.

I didn't even have time to adjust to the emptiness before Harley was bending me over the hood and relentlessly pounding into me again.

I'd be lying if i said we weren't down here for another two hours on top of the hours we spent in her bedroom after she finally decided to stopedging me.

When i woke up i was sore and exhausted.

That woman sure has the stamina of a goddess.

I sat up to find Harley nowhere in sight meaning she was likely in her office doing something.

I headed to her bathroom and took a quick shower throwing on one of her shirts she'd never be getting back.

When i walked back into the room there was a plate of breakfast and apple juice sat on her nightstand with a note.

'I'll be back in less than 10 minutes love, I'm trying to be romantic here. I'd say I hope you enjoy the breakfast but i know you will since im and amazing cook and all. Anyways see you soon.

I love you, Love, Harley'

My girl is such a dork but she sure knows how to make me smile

I can't believe we're on 'I love you' terms. Seems like it was just last week i was regretting not getting off that plane

I caught myself staring at the note and cheesing at myself like a weirdo so I climbed back under her duvet and finished the omelet just as Harley got back to the apartment

She was trying to be sneaky and rush pass the bedroom but i caught her.

"Get in here dork" I playfully rolled my eyes and patted the spot next to me.

Harley slowly entered the room with her hands behind her back in attempt to hide something.

"What's that you're hiding behind your back?" Harley pretended to look around the room clueless.

"I have no idea what you're talking about chérie" Her lips formed a playful grin just as she was slowly backing away into the kitchen.

I got up from my spot on the bed and caught up to her by yanking her closer by her shirt

Our faces were now inches apart

Harley was about to lean closer just as i snuck my hand behind her back grabbing the item which appeared to be flowers

Peonies

I gasped in awe and threw myself at her wrapping my legs around her as if she was a tree.

"I love them so much, I love you so much. Thank you" My voice muffled.

She supported my weight and carried me to the kitchen.

"No. Me more." Harley sat me on the island and made her way toward the sink.

"No." I uttered.

Harley began filling a vase with water.

"Yes." She uttered back.

She took the flowers from me and began cutting the stems off of them

"Whatever." I scoffed deciding to admire her instead

I'd rather not go head to head with her right now especially with how persistent she can be.

Harley finished up with the flowers and made her way back over to me in-between my legs

"They'll still be here for you when you come back. Either dead or alive. We'll see." She shrugged

I puckered my lip initiating i wanted a kiss

"My girl is so romantic and thoughtful, Gracias mi amor"

Harley only hummed.

If be lying if i said her energy didn't shift suddenly.

She walked toward her halfway closet opening it retrieve a box.

"Here, i want to give you something." She placed the long rectangular maroon velvet box in my palm.

"Jesus Harley i don't need anymore gifts, you already give so much" She rolled her eyes signaling me to open it.

"Nothing i give you will ever come close to what you deserve so open it" Her voice suddenly became serious.

I followed her orders and lifted the top of the velvet box to reveal a thin necklace with a vibrant blue gem in the middle of it.

"It's my birthstone, Blue sapphire so as long as it's on, you're mine and i'm with you" Her eyes clearly expressing her seriousness.

She took the box out of my palm and picked up the almost fragile looking necklace

She moved my hair to side— putting the necklace on with ease without me having to turn around

I cupped her face eagerly bringing her into a kiss

Harley sighed into the kiss her arms on both sides of my waist

I slightly pulled away "I'll never ever take it off" I promised to her and myself

My girl hummed backing away further—unbuttoning the first few buttons of her blouse revealing an matching necklace with a more neutral looking stone

Harley then spoke "Your birthstone, White Topaz"

"I feel special for being the only reason you wear a necklace" I teased

The woman was barely seen with anything but a watch and a couple of rings but never a necklace

Harley leaned back in clapping her hands in mine as her forehead rested against mine

"You are special."

I could only attempt to hide my blush at her words.

"I love you, Harley Monet" My gaze fixated on hers.

"I love you, Iris Rosado" The words smoothly exited her mouth as if she'd spent days reciting the perfect way to say it.

"Take me to bed?" Harley's face lit up.

"I thought you'd never ask" She picked me up and carried me to the bedroom gently throwing me onto the bed.

I think i should show her what she'd be missing.

Chapter 38

Harley POV

Iris pulled me down by my neck connecting our lips.

Her legs hooked around my waist in no time and our tongues were devouring each other.

Her syrup glazed tongue coaxing mine.

Her soft almost inaudible moans sent shivers down my spine.

To say i would miss this let alone touching her would be an understatement.

I miss her even when she's just peacefully resting or showering.

My thoughts consumed my mind so much i didn't ever realize we'd stop kissing

Iris looked up at me with a staggering and concerned gaze

I knew she wanted to ask me what was wrong but i can't waste anymore time knowing she leaves in approximately 14 hours "i'm fine, don't worry about me let's just enjoy the few hours we have together. No questions or thoughts, just us. Okay?" My girl hummed in agreement pecking my lips once more

"Okay. Speaking of a few more hours together.." She drifted off "Let me please you before i go" Iris mumbled against my lips

I pretended to hum in thought—tucking a lose strand of her long dark hair behind her ear

"You know you don't have to ask chérie" I smirked at the nickname i'd been calling her since day 1

It's unbelievable how she really became my sweetheart; my darling and it was no longer just a word i'd use to be sarcastic but a word to only slightly express my love for her

Iris tugged me down with her—straddling my waist soon after

"What a beautiful view, you, under me for once" She joked

"Don't get used to it." I scoffed resting my hands on her waist keeping her a-steady

"Whatever you say Harley" My gorgeous girl rolled her beautiful brown eyes

"Take of your shirt" She demanded.

"You know, the moroccan in me wouldn't usually comply but fine." I said whilst sitting up and removing my blouse to which Iris helped me unbutton.

She hummed in satisfaction at the reveal of my abs.

"I see them everyday but they never cease to bless my eyes" She seductively licked her lips—gently running her fingers over them.

I carefully took in her perfect features while she was too busy admiring the results of a gym rats hard work "They're all yours" She looked back up locking eyes with me

Iris leaned in—her lips brushing against mine as she said "I know."

Those words instantly awakened something in me and the aching pulse in my vagina was enough proof.

"You gonna do it or not?" I could tell my brow instinctively raised but i was in need of something.

"Rushing me? Because if so i'll only take longer" She questioned.

"Never, my love. Proceed as you were" I waved her off.

"Damn the ultimate teaser can't take it? How cute" She teased me pinching my cheeks

I puffed my cheeks— looking away in annoyance

Iris cutely chuckled as she climbed off of the bed She made me sit up and move closer to edge of the bed immediately unbuttoning and pulling down my trousers.

The last thing to go was my underwear.

I couldn't help but laugh at her sudden aggressiveness though i got silently got scolded for it.

My love sharply spreaded my legs devouring me immediately.

Running her tongue through my folds lapping up any and all types of moisture

Her mouth fully covering my clit as her tongue experimentally swirled circles around it

Her tongue was so soft and her swirls so perfectly gentle i couldn't help but to react to any sudden movement her tongue made

I brought my hand to her head—gently grabbing a handful and successfully bringing her closer

"Use your fingers if you want, use what you want to, okay?" I assured in case she was hesitantly thinking of it

My girl nodded into my core immediately lathering her index and middle finger with her saliva.

She teased my entrance only pushing them in halfway in attempt to get me used to the sudden stretch but it didn't take long until she pushed them inside me knuckle deep.

I couldn't help the throaty moan that escaped from my mouth but fuck.

"I'm sorry baby but you never go easy on me now do you?" Iris seductively looked up holding intense eye contact with me all while she continued finger fucking me.

Just as i was about to respond her pace increased and my hips instinctively bucked—matching the speed of her thrust

"Ah right, you're not going to answer are you?" She teasingly laughed against my inner thigh.

I was now continuously grunting and grinding myself against her hand.

Iris kissed the inside of the thighs slowly itching her way back to my core just in time for me to be close enough to finish.

When she finally reached it she took a slow and deadly lick from the base of her fingers to my clit.

She did this continuously until my walls were starting to pulsate around her fingers.

By now i'd already given up trying to suppress my moans.

Now i was a loud moaning mess.

Iris's tongue expertly flicked at my clit at an impeccable speed bringing my closer and closer by the second.

I could tell my girl was putting her all into her thrust, fingers curled making perfect contact with my g-spot.

Iris now switched between swirling circles around my clit to flicking.

I could've sworn at one point i felt her spelling her name out with her tongue.

"You're doing so good my love, i'm close keep going" I said just as i threw my head back—the angle allowing the moans to escape once more

Just as Iris's mouth cupped my clit and began sucking on it i came undone on her fingers

My fingers painfully tugging at her hair as my legs shook in pleasure.

She removed her fingers and replaced them with her tongue getting anything she could from me.

She slurped and lathered me up 'til there was nothing left for me to give.

She made her way back up to me by leaving little pecks up my body.

When she reached my mouth she closed the distance with a long peck to which i fully relaxed into—allowing myself to fully hum into it as my chest heaved up and down from my climax.

Iris then pulled away placing her fingers inside my mouth allowing myself to taste the sweetness of my come.

I sucked them clean and slowly released them from my mouth.

"I should've done that more often" My girl said as she threw herself beside me with her face smothered in my neck.

I softly chuckled as i brought my hand up and ran it through her straight silky locs of hair.

Theres more time my love, you're next.

Chapter 39

Iris POV

"All packed up my love?" Harley asked me as i zipped up my suitcase and stood with it.

I hummed and nodded as she took it out of my hand and rolled it to the front door.

A sudden wave of dread washed over me and my heart began feeling heavy.

Even though i made it sound like i was perfectly fine with long distance doesn't mean i was on the inside.

I've never been in a relationship before and i don't know what our dynamic will be once we're away more than we can handle.

What if i can't bare going too long without her touch or her lips on mine or just even her scent.

Im not one to overthink but i really want this to work and I'm hopeful it will but, you can never be too sure how life will go.

Harley sat next me on her now freshlymade up bed

Her arms slithered around my waist—pulling me closer to which my head instinctively found her shoulder in no time

Harley was holding me differently. Not to be romantic but to reassure me.

"The more you dread and think of it the harder the situation will become. Just let it be and fall into place, no matter what happens i'm not letting you go. You're the one for me and we'll always find a way to each other, i know i will." Her words gentle and covered in sincerity

"I know." I could only speak so much right now. I just wanted to get the hard part over with

Harley could only sigh at the dullness of my mood right now but i knew she understood

She brought my hand up to her lips placing a gentle kiss on them "Te amo Iris, eres mi todo."

"I love you, Harley. Always." I lifted my head just enough to be able to kiss her

Her tongue hesitantly entering my mouth as if she didn't want to get too carried away

I shifted my position so that i was straddling her with my hands tangled in her long curly hair

Harley eventually laid back on the bed allowing me to take control of the kiss

She knew this wasn't something sexual to me but something vulnerable. The kiss was telling her something i couldn't put into words

We continued to take our time slowly making out—her fingers softly running up and down my back as our tongues made contact and danced together in a slow dance

This went on for minutes until the sound of my alarm went off

Harley reached behind me pulling my phone out of my back pocket silencing the alarm all while continuing the kiss me

She threw my phone to the side and sat up with me still straddling her lap.

She broke the kiss—making her way up my jaw.

When she reached near my ear she finally spoke "I guess it's time" She practically said to herself.

"I can always miss my flight" I joked.

Harley made sure i saw her roll her eyes "Very funny. You know how much i'd love that but you'd never do it now would you?" Her left eyebrow perked in fake curiosity.

I shook my head—finally standing and breaking physical contact with my girl.

She stood after me and began grabbing a jacket and her keys.

"I'm going to take your bags to the car, take your time okay?" She kissed my temple and made her way down to the garage soon after

Such a gentlewoman.

I quickly made my way to the bathroom and splashed water on face

This was going to be a long ass flight and i'd definitely be experiencing jet lag again with the time change.

At least this time i'd be comfortable, my girl strictly instructed i take her jet instead of some other airline so i'd be more 'comfortable' but i knew she just wanted the power of being able to track where i am during the entire flight

I figured i was taking too long in the bathroom and made my way out of it toward the front door but not before saying goodbye to Harley's cat who i'd miss so much

Maybe i'd get myself one back in Texas

Rory would love that

Speaking of the kid she'd be visiting soon and i'd really need to get my life together by then.

My thoughts were interrupted by the ding of the elevator.

I'd reached her overly large garage and made my way toward my girlfriend who had been leaning against the hood of her Jeep waiting for me while on a phone call to which i only slightly overheard.

"Ecoutez, je dois y aller mais dites-lui de garder ses gens loin de moi. Je ne veux pas faire partie de cette merde. Papa ou pas." With that she hung up.

"Ready chérie?" She shoved her phone in her pocket and rounded the car— opening the door for me

"Mhm, who was that?" I curiously asked

"Just some of my dads dumbass coworkers, nothing to worry about" She closed the door and made her way to the drivers side

"Your dad? You never talk about him" I continued as she entered the car

"Because he only comes around when he needs something from me, that's not a very sincere relationship now is it?" She rhetorically asked as she put on her seatbelt

"I guess" I mumbled as i did the same deciding not to carry on with the topic.

The ride to the airport was silent with the radio on low volume and our hands engulfed in one anothers the entire ride.

Within 40 minutes we were pulling into the private area of the airport.

Harley pulled up beside the jet and got out of the car to hand my bags to the attendant when she re-entered the car she leaned over pulling me in for another short kiss to which i reciprocated.

"What was that for?" I mumbled against her lips.

"Nothing my love" She pulled away— regaining her position.

"Let's get you onto that jet before i lock you in my car" She half joked as she came around to open my door

"I wish you could just come with me" I whined as she guided me inside the jet

"Soon, baby." She softly kissed my temple

When i stepped onto the jet i was shook. It was modern and definitely screamed rich.

Cream leather seats with golden and brown accents all around the aircraft

My jaw subconsciously dropped in awe.

"Your purchases never fail to shock me" I said as i began looking around the aircraft.

Harley sat down in one of the seats slightly slouching "This is nothing my love, nothing compared to what i'd give you" She spoke as she began rapidly typing on her phone.

Choosing to ignore it; i continued looking around.

"Oh hush i'd never accept anything this extravagant and who casually has a whole bathroom covered in Dior essentials" I scoffed as i made my way to the seat across from her.

"What can i say, i'm a girl with expensive taste" She smirked as she adjusted herself and began manspreading

We talked about everything and anything until the pilot stepped onto the jet

Harley stood and introduced us

"This is our pilot, Auclair, Pilot Auclair this is my girlfriend Iris" Her arm resting over my shoulder

"Nice to meet you Iris I'll be your pilot for today, i hope you enjoy the flight" He spoke in a very thick french accent as he shook my hand

He looked to Harely "Nous partons bientôt"

She nodded and looked at him intensely "Prends soin de ma copine Auclair, je pense que tu sais ce qui arrivera si tu ne le fais pas, hm?"

I had no fucking idea what was going on but it definitely inserted some sort of fear into him for him to only nod his head and hurriedly make his way inside the cockpit.

"What did you say to him Harley" I glared at her.

"Don't look at me that way you know i like it" She pecked my lips guiding me to a seat on the plane and making me buckle up.

"Nothing too serious, we're friends" I could tell she was half joking if her smirk was an indication.

"On a serious note, you're leaving in a couple of minutes so i have to leave but text me as much as you can and rest okay? Call me when you land my love. I love you so much" She covered my face in kisses.

Our last moments went by in a blur.

From me watching her step off the craft to me watching her slowly wave at me from her car as the jet drove toward the runway.

i could've sworn i seen her wiping her eyes but i could be wrong.

The lights dimmed as we finally took off.

I couldn't hold onto my emotions anymore. I let them all lose as cardigan played in my ear.

I allowed the tears the fall freely until i cried myself to sleep.

And that's the story of how Harley Monet became my prophecy, my way of living, my heart.

Chapter 40

Harley POV

I stared at my phone sitting on the kitchen counter—waiting for any indication of a call or text or any fucking sign of her

It's been 4 months since she left and to say things went downhill from there

The first 2 months were great, we'd call every night and text throughout the day to inform each other about our whereabouts

Everything was smooth and it didn't even feel like the distance affected us or at all— Until a couples of weeks ago Iris told me she'd be going to a work dinner—I had no thoughts about it i just hoped she'd enjoy herself. I even got intimate pictures out of it for helping her decide on a dress to wear to the event

Last minute i decided to surprise her and showed up at the dinner party. When i arrived the sight of her boss she'd previously told me had a little crush on her and tried to make subtle moves on her—to which she declined had her fucking arm around my girls waist

Flashback

Goodness this is what i walk into? Not even a minute i'd been in the ballroom and I'm met with the souring sight of another woman touching my woman

I stood back a couple more seconds to see if Iris would shove her off or do at least something about it—I could tell she was trying to disguise how uncomfortable she was just by how she was laughing and slowly moving away

Deciding i'd had enough of it i walked up to the group just as Iris unhooked the woman's arm and excused herself—as she turned around we were finally met with the sight of one another—after a mere 3 months of being apart

Iris's captivating dark brown siren eyes held shock as we took each other in; She was wearing an ankle length black dress with a deep cleavage slit and leg slit revealing almost her entire leg—I could tell she was contemplating on whether or not to jump on me or hold her composure to which she settled on a searing kiss i could barely reciprocate

She took notice and immediately pulled back—looking at me in shock. I was about to say something until i noticed her cunt of a boss staring at us so, i did what any sane person would do and i rightfully pulled my girl in by the waist with one arm and used my free hand to pull her in by the neck all while keeping eye contact with the woman whose name i didn't even know

Iris's arms wrapped around my neck as our tongues painfully consumed each other after so long—I again could barely enjoy it because i was too focused on proving that she was mine

This was once more a short lived kiss as Iris pulled back "What the fuck Harley!? Why are you kissing me like that" She harshly whispered

"Oh don't fucking give me that as if you didn't just have another woman's arms around yourwaist" I said in all attempts not to be aggressive toward her with my words—I never want to put her in a position to where i yell at her—especially publicly

Iris's gaze dropped to the floor as if she wasn't aware i'd seen their interaction. She looked around and took notice that a couple of people were staring and took my hand and led us to a singular family sized bathroom right outside of the ballroom

I didn't even have time to take in how fancy it was before i was brought back to reality by the sound of her locking the door

"I pulled her arm away okay? Lyn can be very pushy and touchy but i don't know how to stop her..she's so consistent with it no matter how much i push her away and tell her im with you—I don't want to be rude about it because i have to see her everyday at work and she could possibly fire me" Iris said all in one breath as she walked toward me as I leaned against the dark marble sink with my arms crossed

"I'll fucking solve it for you" I mumbled under my breath

Iris looked at me as if she was waiting for me to say more

"I could give a shit about you hurting her feelings what about mine? Have you taken that into consideration Iris?" I looked away from her as my jaw ticked in frustration

Iris placed her hand over mine in attempt to say something as a knock on the door cut her off—Deciding the conversation should just be postponed until we got to her house i pecked her on the cheek

I leaned into her ear and whispered "We'll talk about this more later but if she pulls that shit again tonight don't be surprised if i handle it myself" and with that i walked to the door and opened it to reveal the woman i now knew as Lyn

"Ah it's you" She grinned "Nice to meet you i've heard so much about you" She then held her hand out in hopes i'd shake it

I only glared at her and made my way past her ensuring i bumped her shoulder hard enough to make her stumble and made my way back toward the ballroom with Iris following behind

When we made our way back they were just beginning to announce awards—Iris was placed at a table with a couple of her friends to which i introduced myself to and joined the table since there were a couple of empty seats

Things were fine and at ease until of course—Lyn was miraculously placed at the same table as us and decided to sit right next to Iris

It took everything in me not to say something but Iris's gentle caresses on my thigh kept me sane

For awhile.

Up until Iris was called up for an award to which we all stood and congratulated her—Iris made her way up front and accepted the award and did a little 'thank you' speech

When Iris made her way back to the table and sat; Lyn took it upon herself to place her hand on my girls thigh and lean in for a kiss on the cheek all while holding eye contact with me—she made sure i knew her intentions and saw everything but that'd be one of her biggest mistakes

It's like something finally clicked in my head

All the fuzz and frustration finally consumed me and i just exploded—blacked out.

I had no idea what i was doing until i heard a couple of people scream in shock and the sound of my girls voice begging me to get off of her

I then realized Lyn was under me holding her bloodied and likely broken nose; Her eyebrow was busted along with her lip which was more swollen than ever and I was holding a shard of glass up to her throat from a wine glass i apparently smashed against the table

My god what was i doing? Acting like some fucking possessive lunatic with no self control—surely i was scaring the shit out of Iris and her coworkers

Je deviens exactement ce que mon père veut que je devienne

Realizing i should leave before someone called the cops i stood and reached for a cloth on the table and wiped my hands free of her blood

Fucking shit my knuckles are bruised up and purple

I then threw the dirtied cloth at Lyn who was whaling like a little girl on the ground—still holding her nose in pain

"Clean yourself up and stay away from my girlfriend so this won't have to happen again alright?" I spoke as she only looked at me in disgust

"Right" I mumbled under my breath

"I think it's time for us to leave Iris, let's go" I then finally turned to her to see a look in her eyes i couldn't decipher but it wasn't very happy

Iris scoffed and angrily turned around making her way out of the ballroom—the sound of her heels filled the room you'd think was empty but everyone was in too much shock to say or do anything

So much for a surprise visit.

End

After that whole interaction we got into a big fight in the car on the way to her house and i just decided to go back home

The very next day she texted me that she got fired and i of course felt bad but she didn't exactly need a job anyway. She has me and i couldn't stomach the thought of her working for that bitch anymore

After Iris told me she got fired she began ignoring me—going as far as not answering text or calls and i was going fucking crazy

I'd gotten so used to talking to her all the time that being alone again felt so surreal and out of the ordinary and i'd honestly just been hopeful for something as little as a phone call and that she wasn't going to break up with me

As if i'd allow that.

I decided that if she was going to continue to ignore me i'd just show up at her house tomorrow morning. Atleast this time she'd be at home and i couldn't necessarily hurt anyone and this time i was going to make it right and fix our fucking relationship.

I'm sure if i'd just stayed that night and talked it out like Iris wanted me to things wouldn't be how they are.

Curse my parents for giving me a lack of communication and stubbornness.

I spent all night packing and convincing myself it was a good idea and by morning i was on my jet making my way to Texas

I sent her a couple of text just to see if she'd acknowledge them to which she didn't and i suddenly began overthinking

My god what if she isn't even home when I get there?

No she will be i'll arrive around night time

What if she turns me around and refuses to listen to me?

No she will. I still have to try and overthinking it won't help anything—i'm already on the goddamn plane and there's no going back now

I sighed and leaned my head against the window and opted to sleep as much as i could

When i woke up it was a few minutes until landing meaning i slept way over 8 hours which was a miracle seeing as i hadn't been sleeping since she started abruptly ignoring me.

When i finally landed i wasted no time driving to her house and when i finally parked i just sat there.

What do i even say to her? Do i apologize? I've never really had to do that before but for her I'm willing, I love her.

I just need her to talk to me before i actually go insane.

I pulled down the car mirror and looked at myself

My hair wasn't as luscious and lively as it was before, my eyes have become darker and duller from stress

I puffed out my cheeks as i mentally prepared myself for what was about to come

Is this really what love does to you? Not just affect you mentally but physically? So bad to the point you don't even look like yourself? I couldn't even fathom the idea of it before but look at me now—so crazy for someone everything they do affects me.

I can't even look at myself for too long without feeling the disappointment i've brought upon myself and the situation and i couldn't bare sitting in this car any longer while i criticized myself.

Stepping out of the rental car felt like i was carrying the weight of the world on my back or maybe that was just the guilt.

Why was i so damn terrified of my own girlfriend who might not even be my girlfriend anymore?

The walk to her door felt like an eternity and when i finally lifted my wrist to knock on the door it opened abruptly without warning

"Ugh finally you were sitting in the car like a lunatic—i was staring to think you were never going to get out" Rory mumbled

"Rory?" I stood shocked

I thought she was supposed to be back home by now

"What? I thought you were some weird burgler at first until i realized it was you" She shrugged

"I'm glad you're here though you two really need to talk.. I'll go get her stay here" Rory slammed the door and i could hear her yelling at Iris—telling her she had a guest

Iris's voice echoed closer to the door second by second and by each second my heart thumbed louder and my palms grew sweatier and sweatier

"A guest? I'm not expecting—" Her sentence cut short at the sight at me

She stared at me in shock until Rory cleared her throat and announced she was going to be upstairs

"Me tendiste una trampa, pequeña rata." Iris turned to yell at Rory as she hurriedly made her way up the stairs

When she finally turned to me she widened the door and took in my entire appearance to which i felt horrible about which is a rare occurrence for me

"Iris." I said in hopes she'd say something and acknowledge me

My girl looked up and deeply exhaled

Harley

Chapter 41

Iris POV

She looked horrible. Her hair was a mess and untamed which was very out of the usual from her usual clean and tamed look. Now she just looked like some depressed teenager who'd been rotting in their bedroom all day. She even started wearing hoodies, she never wears hoodies!

According to her, it takes away from her matureness and elegance. So much for that now.

Just as I was about to invite her in her stomach growled

"Jesus Harley, are you even taking care of yourself? Get in here" I pulled her inside by her hoodie causing her to stumble forward

"Still strong I see" She mumbled and placed her suitcase to the side as I closed and locked the door

I pointed toward the dinner table "Sit." To which she complied

"And—ugh stop looking at me like that" I grumbled as I made my way to the kitchen

She's been making eye contact with me the entire time—silently communicating something to which I don't even know what that is! But it was driving me crazy and making me feel guilty and it wasn't the time to be feeling those things especially before we talk

I began taking out ingredients to make her favorite meal from home—Moroccan Pastilla

As I turned around I literally fucking screamed; Harley suddenly appeared of nowhere and was leaning on the kitchen island watching me gather ingredients. I hadn't even heard her get up let alone walk this way

"Ouch?" She said sarcastically in response to my scream

Why the fuck hadn't Rory run down here yet? What if I was dying or something

I rolled my eyes and began searching for the recipe instructions I wrote down as soon as she told me it was her favorite dish months ago

Harley stood up straight and began making her way around the island "Do you ever listen? I told you to sit at the table" I said with an ounce of fake annoyance—I honestly didn't mind her watching me, I found it comforting but I'm still a little mad at her to express that.

As I was reaching for the pepper flakes on the top shelf I felt no other than Harley's body against mine—I was now locked in between her and the counter

She moved my hair to one side of my shoulder now exposing my neck to which she shortly began leaving small kisses on

"I've missed you" She whispered—her voice raspy as she wrapped her arms around my waist—hugging me from behind

I couldn't help but gulp at how easy it was for her to ignite any type of heat inside me

Why was i fucking horny from a simple whisper!?

No. I can't give in to her so easily no matter how effortlessly sexy she is

I cleared my throat and turned around in her arms slightly shoving her away "Why don't you be helpful and grab the pepper flakes for me?"

She only smirked and nodded leaning in closer than before—inches away from my face

I closed my eyes preparing for her to kiss me but was shortly disappointed when I felt her placing the bottle in my hand causing me to finally open my eyes

"The pepper flakes you requested my love" Harley chuckled at the state I was previously in

I frowned and mumbled a 'Thanks' and moved past her toward the island and began cutting the chicken almost appreciating the silence

"You know if you want a kiss all you have to do is ask" She challengingly said and she leaned against the island again only this time she was leaning against her hand and making intense eye contact with me to which I was avoiding

"I don't." I quickly muttered

"Right." Harley hummed

"And i don't have to ask. You're mine." I added as I glared at her which only made her smirk

"Hm so we are still together? Good to know" She let out a sigh of relief and made her way next to me and began helping me prepare the meal for her

How the hell did she come to that conclusion? I didn't break up with the girl i just...gave her the silent treatment for a while as punishment. "Did i say we weren't? I don't know where else you'd get the idea from fight or not."

"You ignored me for weeks!" She damn near hissed "Even then you're not allowed to break up with me, you're in it for life darling" She chuckled to herself as she placed the dish in the oven

"In it for..life? What does that even mean" I questioned her choice of words

"Nothing. Now can we talk while the pastilla is in the oven?" I sighed and nodded and led her toward the living room

She sat on one end and I sat on the other

What have we come to? We couldn't even keep our hands off each other in Paris now we're a foot apart.

Harley silently took in the place and shifted in her spot until she got comfortable

"Nice place you've got, It's very.. you"

"Very me? Meaning?" I said defensively

She nodded "Its dark and minimalistic, it fits you, i like it" She justified as i side eyed her

I hummed and began fiddling with my fingers not sure what to say "So what brings you here?" I questioned. Why the fuck is it so awkward

Her brow perked at my question "Well i just came to visit my girl and find out why she's been avoiding me"

"Hm i don't know maybe because you got me fired" I emphasized fired

She scoffed "Yes but she deserved it did she not?" She said nonchalantly as if it didn't affect her at all

I stood and began walking up the stairs—ending the conversation "Whatever Harley." If she wasn't going to take the conversation seriously i wasn't going to continue it.

Seconds later i heard her hurried footsteps running up the stairs after me "Okay okay i'm sorry i'll be serious" She was now panting and out of breath

There's no way the Harley I know is panting over 10 steps

"Sure you are" I pushed past her and made my way inside my room with Harley obviously following behind me—I was caught off guard when she grabbed my wrist and held them above my head pinning me against the door

She rested her forehead against mine stared into my eyes "I'll apologize for getting you fired and maybe acting immature but i wont apologize for being protective and possessive over you. She clearly wanted what was mine and couldn't take the hint—for fuck sake she was disrespecting us let alone you so I handled it, that I'm not sorry for, I'm not sorry for caring" She whispered the last part to herself

She had a point. She just didn't need to blatantly punch her in front of everyone

"Plus I don't want you working for someone who wants to fuck you anyway." Her eye twitched as she said that "Unless it's me of course" She bit her lip at the thought

"I'm sorry for ignoring you for weeks, very unnecessary and immature. When don't know how to deal with conflict ignoring the entire situation is my number one solution so i'm sorry. I won't do it again those weeks were hell without you and I can tell they were for you too if your physical state is any indication" I mumbled the last part to myself

"Damn right they were hell, do you see what i'm wearing? You know life's getting to me when you see me wearing a hoodie" She chuckled "I'll be back to normal in a couple of days, I need to catch up on some sleep first" Harley groaned

She then released my wrist "Can i kiss you now?" She questionably tilted her head slightly smirking

"Harley what did I say—" I was cut off by a harsh tug forward on my hips—her hands met my ass and I was soon met with her soft lips leading mine in a firm and very needy kiss which would definitely lead to something if we continued any longer but I couldn't bring myself to stop and neither could she

Harley picked me up—my legs instinctively wrapping around her waist as she led me to my bed—My fingers were tangled in her hair as she laid down with me on top of her with her hands still on my ass as I tried to remove her hoodie only to be cut off by a screaming Rory

"What the hell are you burning Iris!?" She shouted down the hallway

Fuck I forgot she was here.

Epilogue

2 Years Later

Rory POV

I began paddling a little further out to where the water had a higher tide.

I needed to ride a large enough wave to feel something and the waves today closer to shore weren't it doing it for me.

The water was glistening, clear, and blue so i could see all sorts of wildlife under me which i couldn't help but admire.

I gathered my dark soaked hair and brought it to one side of my shoulder and began ringing it out to pass the time until the waves built up enough to satisfy me.

I was suddenly caught off guard by the feeling of something brushing against my foot.

What the fuck was that?

Just as i was about the freak out a baby dolphin poked its head out from under my surfboard and began clicking in excitement

"Jesus little one you fucking scared me" I let out a sigh of relief "I thought you were a shark or something" I chuckled to myself reaching down to rub the melon of the dolphin half the size of my board. He began clicking even louder as i was doing so. He truly couldn't be more than a few days old

Where was his mother? I hope she's near but she couldn't have been

Just when i looked up in search for any sign of another dolphin i was caught off guard by a wave and I was immediately pushed underwater and caught in an undertow causing me to stay as calm as i could and swim parallel before it was clear enough for me to resurface and just as i was about to swim back up to the surface the same juvenile dolphin began swimming around me in circles making the same clicking sound

Is something wrong? Should i be worried about something?

The dolphin started brushing against me again—worrying me. I know they're typically friendly animals but they're not usually this close to shore and approachable to humans

Maybe he's trying to tell me something?

I didn't have time to think about it any longer, i was running out of breath and i doubt the dolphin would be able to do anything about that so began swimming up to the surface and looking around for my board. It was only a couple of feet away so i swam toward it and sat back on top of it annoyed at myself for missing the biggest wave of the day

The sun was just beginning to set and i'd have to make my way back home but i could stay for awhile and watch the sunset and that's exactly what i did

During the duration of the sun setting all i could think about was that dolphin. Calf babies are hardly left alone without a mother but he was. The mother—She couldn't be near because she wouldn't have allowed him to get that close to me without showing up

I'm not even sure if the dolphin is a 'he' but regardless he worried me

For fuck sakes why am i overthinking about a dolphin? If anything's wrong i'll alert the coast guard and they'll handle it.

I sighed and made my way back toward shore. So much for surfing today. That wave, It fucking engulfed me and brought me down with it damn near killing me but whatever

When i reached shore i stepped out of my wetsuit, dried off and began walking home.

It was only the end of July and school would be starting in a couples of weeks and i still had loads to do but that isn't my main concern right now

I still have a week to further enjoy the Hawaiian beach life until we moved back into our house in the city

Harley really went all out when it came to living comfortably as she'd put it, buying both a beach house for the summer and main house in the middle of the city for when the summer was over and we'd be back to our everyday lives.

I'd been living with them for a year now—life has really been up and down these past two years more down than anything but i've been getting through it

To say living with Harley and Iris was an upgrade from in El salvador was an understatement, besides their unnecessary fights and occasional noisy nights i loved the new life i was given the opportunity to live

Schools here were better and just the lifestyle overall was less depressing—made me really appreciate nature more

I'd even took it upon myself to discover hidden places and use them as my own little hideout when i needed a break from the world

I sometimes hated how much i've changed over the short years but with all the shit i've endured you'd be surprised if i hadn't. I especially hated how less i'd become a people person day by day

The more people fucked me over and treated me like shit the more the imaginary wall build up inside me—It was now more difficult for me to let people in who weren't my closest family and even then i wasn't as quirky as i used to be but Iris just reassured me that's what came with age so i just let it go

Before i moved here with Iris and Harley they'd just only moved here themselves but were more than happy to take care of me especially with how her parents couldn't care for me anymore, they wanted to enjoy their last years together and i refused to go back home to my 'parents'.

So i moved here and began living the tropical life i've grown to love so much. I transferred in the middle of the year and was closed off from mostly everyone who even attempted to befriend me or peruse me. I was never allowing myself to date someone who went to school with me ever again. We all know how that went back in El Salvador and that bitch ruined my life good enough for me to still be traumatized from it.

Plus, i loved too hard anyway. I'm sure it'd become so strong i'd scare them away so i had zero intentions of getting distracted by any girls

Now, i just had to get through my last year of high school and i'd be officially living the adult life.

Yay me.

After 7 minutes of walking i finally reached the back of our beach house and sat my board against the wall and rinsed off any possible sand off my body and made my way inside

When i walked a bit further into the house I looked around for my now guardians and there they were on the couch cuddling up binging Rebelde

I cleared my throat gaining their attention "That's fucking disgusting" I mumbled to myself to which they looked up at me

"Finally, i thought a shark finally got to you or something" No other than Harley joked

"Maybe one day" I darkly joked back gaining a glare from Iris "Don't say that you rata" I shrugged making my way up the stairs to which Iris yelled out to wash up and that dinner would me ready when i was finished to which i sent her a thumbs up and finally entered my room

To say my room was low key emo was an understatement but what can i say, i love the color black. Any artificial coloring just blinds me and gave me a headache

My wall was covered in posters varying from musical artist such as the Arctic Monkeys, Nirvana, Pierce the veil you name it and a couple of film posters varying from Nana, The outsiders, many Tim Burton posters and just a bunch of other things i loved

My room was slightly messy right now with a couple of clothes scattered on the floor

I had plants scattering my walls along with vinyls with my blood red electric guitar sitting in the corner

Maybe i should get back into that.

I also had a balcony which gave me a side view of the ocean i'd sometimes sit out on late at night listening to as i smoked a blunt

The sound of the waves gently clashing against each other helped me feel a sense of serene and relief i definitely required more than any normal person would

If i forced myself to be around people more than i could handle i'd probably act harshly toward them or simply ignore them.

I groaned to myself as i realized how tired i was and was soon placing the Nana soundtrack vinyl in my record player and began straightening up my room as i hummed to the song

When i finished it took a much needed shower and washed my body and hair free of god knows what germs and within no time i was exiting the shower—catching myself in the mirror

I took some time to admire my features—from my dark wet hair evenly thrown over my shoulders to my just as dark brows to my chocolate brown eyes to my pink full lips

I was starting to realize i wasn't a baby anymore, my usual high and chubby cheeks replaced with my now slender and defined cheeks which matched with my sharp dark features

Maybe it was because i worked out so much i mean—i did workout at least 5 times a week

That would explain my toned tummy which were showing slightly visible abs i'd have to work out more for if i wanted them to be more defined

Deciding against checking myself out any longer i grabbed my toothbrush and brushed my teeth for the night before getting dressed in grey sweats and a plain black tee and headed downstairs for dinner to which Iris and Harley had this thing where if they could—they'd always make dinner together which i did find adorable, perhaps admirable but i'd never admit that to them. I didn't need them calling me sappy.

I took my usual seat and scrolled on my phone as i waited to be served dinner by the couple

"Took you long enough" Iris said as she placed a plate full of spaghetti down in front of me and where Harley would usually sit

They were so weird. They'd only bring plates for each other but never themselves

"A girl has to do what she has to do" I shrugged my shoulders and mumbled a 'thanks' as i brought the fork up to my mouth feeling satisfied with the flavors

"I'm assuming Harley took the lead tonight with dinner" I said with a mouthful of spaghetti as they both sat down—Harley across from me and Iris next to her

Iris frowned at my comment "No, i did you ass" She scoffed causing Harley to chuckle

I hummed taking a sip of water "That Moroccan Pastilla you tried to make says other wise" I muttered back furthermore stuffing my face with spaghetti

"Oh my god give me a break that was so long ago and plus, I was preoccupied" Iris nodded gaining a smirk out of Harley

Ew?

"Yeah i think i'm done with dinner for the night" I fake gagged causing them to laugh at my disgust as i made my toward the kitchen placing my dish in the sink and headed upstairs shouting a 'goodnight' over the balcony before i resided in my room for the night

Once i enter my room there's no telling when you'll see me again, when it comes to school breaks i practically lived in my room and cut myself off from any and all human interaction, i guess i just hate the human race that much but what normal person doesn't every once in a while?

I know i do more than i should but i don't care enough to do anything about it, it's not like there's anyone who's even came close to getting me out of my ways and i doubt anyone ever would anytime soon

I was getting bored of being bored ironic enough and scrolling on my phone all the time so i further decided to learn a couple of songs on my electric guitar and did my usual smoking a blunt and listening to the waves crash into each other daily routine

After that i just laid in bed—staring up at the ceiling stuck in my thoughts which consisted of random shit like my dread of the start of school and just my day overall.

Wait that dolphin—what the hell was that about?

I let my curiosity get the best of me and reached for my laptop on the opposite side of my bed and began looking for any possible answers like 'What does it mean when a newborn dolphin is left alone' and if there was any spiritual meaning behind it and you best believe there was

According to some random website dolphins were a sign of good luck and..love? They're considered love messengers and are linked with aphrodite..and they apparently helped people reach their true love.

This couldn't have applied to me what so ever.

What makes the universe think i'm looking for fucking love?

I then threw my laptop on the opposite end of my bed and laid back down harshly tossing and turning in attempts to fall asleep but i just couldn't get myself to.

Not with what that website said about my interaction today

Who could possibly want to love me? What makes the universe even think me and that 'L' word even belonged together in the same sentence?

Me and 'true love'? Nah, Wrong Rory.